Poseidon's Legacy

By
David C. Dagley

Strategic Book Publishing
www.sbpra.net

For information about special discounts for bulk purchases, please contact Strategic Book Publishing, Special Sales, at bookorder@sbpra.net.

ISBN: 978-1-68235-614-2

Inspired by Nicole Kuhn

'A Wizard of the Sea'

1

Two figures stood in the wheelhouse swaying to the rhythm of the sea as the captain maneuvered his fishing boat into position. Red ambers dangled from their clove cigarettes. Small waves washed over a nearby shallow reef. It was almost slack tide, slowing to a pause, and then it would retreat. Beyond the reef, a low atoll broke the surface with moonlit grass languidly bending in the breeze. The silhouette of a lone tree, stunted by years of scorching sun, sea spray, and monsoon winds stood above a bleached coral beach.

The deckhand moved aft to grab a line connected to a trailing dugout canoe and hauled it alongside the fishing boat to tie it off. The captain walked over carrying a cardboard box with a plastic liner taped shut and passed it to his deckhand, who set it in the middle of the canoe. Both men turned their attention to a bulky roll of custom sewn fishing net laced with large stainless steel hooks all rolled on an aluminum spool. They shouldered the spool to the stern rail and struggled to place it in its stocks. The deckhand tossed a coil of leader line into the canoe and attached it to a cleat at the back. Metal pipe clamps and industrial strength strong-ties fastened the net to a thin metal cable lined with sealed plastic water bottle buoys. The captain rolled an upright rusty blue oil drum to the edge of the spool. He used a stick to stir the coagulating blood saturating the bait balls one last time. The putrid stench filled the captain's nostrils and made his eyes water. The deckhand got in the canoe and pushed the cardboard box further away with his feet before untying from the fishing boat. As the canoe moved toward the atoll, the captain meticulously let out net, pointing a penlight at the roll to make sure the hooks weren't catching on the net mesh below. He attached bait balls to hooks randomly. It was a slow and painstaking process done under a curtain of darkness. As the canoe approached the reef, the deckhand whistled back to the captain who stopped letting out net. The deckhand untied the leader line from his canoe and began letting it out to keep the net in deeper water. The canoe scraped and broke staghorn coral spikes as it made its way across the shallow reef to the beach. While there was still a slight current, the captain opened a cooler of more decaying fish and blood, and retrieved more bait balls attached to one meter of line and a plastic buoy bottle. He began throwing the bait balls into the water. The bait balls splashed down and sank while the bottles reflected fractured moonlight on the surface.

The deckhand got out of his canoe and walked onto the beach, still letting out leader line one coil at a time. He scrambled up the bleached coral bank to the weathered tree and wrapped the line around its base and tied it off. The deckhand could barely see his canoe rocking in the moonlight as it drifted with the breeze and current. Phosphorescent green algae tumbled in the small surf washing over the reef and turned the canoe sideways, keeping it close to shore. He grabbed hold of the canoe rail and began guiding it back out beyond the reef. He opened his box, cut the plastic liner and began throwing bait balls in the sea to scent the water where the net dangled into the deep. He took a moment to wash his hands and the sweat off his face before climbing into the canoe and paddling quietly toward the fishing boat. The captain's bait buoys bobbed in the current, slowly moving toward the net as the deckhands' buoyed bait balls moved away. The deckhand threw the blood-soaked cardboard box and plastic bag into the sea after all the bait balls had been tossed. Returning to the fishing boat, they began letting out the remaining net. The captain moved to the wheelhouse and engaged the engine to slowly make way. The net fell off the rolling spool and unfolded into the darkness with weights attached at the bottom. The tide stopped for a few moments before it began to churn in all directions. Water boiled up from the deep and whirlpools formed sucking the surface water down their center. The captain used the boat engine to keep the net taut and straight while the current changed direction. When all was in place both men sat in the wheelhouse and smoked clove cigarettes waiting for their prey. They finished their smokes and the captain prepared four sticks of dynamite with packets of ball bearings and rusty nails taped around the middle of the sticks to ensure the appropriate impact. He placed four sticks in a plastic container with two lighters and clasped the lid shut. He handed the container to his deckhand who got in the canoe with the container in his lap. The captain grabbed two large plastic containers of cyanide and handed them into the canoe along with another lit cigarette. They smoked and spoke quietly together, waiting patiently while watching the tide and the buoyed net begin to arc in the opposite direction. The captain periodically adjusted his course and grabbed more bait balls with no buoys attached and threw into whirlpools hoping to draw his prize out of the deep. The setup had gone as planned. He double-checked his dynamite stock, his cyanide containers, and his harpoon with a long lead attached to a cleat at the port stern quarter of the boat near the outboard engines.

They sat under the moonlight and watched the surface water and buoys for activity. The Milky Way surrounded them in a carpet of stars. The grass on the atoll continued to press in the wind and swells crossed the sea. Outlines of distant islands flashed under lightning strikes on volcanic mountaintops. Everything seemed silver and black as small ripples lapped against the hull.

An hour passed before the net tugged downward and shook violently. The captain stood up and watched the action for a moment, then sat back down not interested in something that size. It could have been a shark or a humphead wrasse but it wasn't his prize. The two men smoked another cigarette as the animal entangled itself. The net took a second jolting hit and five buoys submerged. The net swung as a creature tried to break free. The deckhand held on to the fishing boat rail, ready to go out and finish the task. The captain watched as the net continued to move back and forth. The captain waved off the deckhand and throttled up to keep the net from folding. The deckhand paddled into the current and began pouring cyanide in the water as he went. The cyanide drifted down on an intercept course for the creature. The captain lit a fuse of dynamite and threw it above the unseen animal. The deckhand back-paddled, watching the water and waiting for the explosion. The captain threw another stick of dynamite and the deckhand opened his plastic box as the first stick of dynamite flashed and boiled to the surface. The deckhand lit a stick and dropped it in the water. The current drew the canoe closer to the thrashing net. The third stick of dynamite exploded twenty meters below the surface and the net stopped moving. All the buoys returned to the surface along with a school of dead fish. The captain and his deckhand watched and waited, each with a stick of dynamite at the ready. The captain signaled the deckhand to move closer and look. The deckhand turned his canoe sideways as he approached the net. He peered into the water holding a torch and examined the net from the surface. The canoe suddenly flipped over. The captain watched in horror as his deckhand disappeared and all went still. Panicked, the captain turned and hurriedly opened a jug of cyanide and poured it around the stern of his boat as a precaution before throwing two sticks of dynamite, one on each side of the net. He watched the capsized canoe as it drifted over the net with only a portion of the hull glistening under the stars. Down below, the two sticks of dynamite exploded and flashed, again sending boiling streams of bubbles to the surface. The captain watched the net from the stern with his boat still in gear. He noticed the boat was swinging off course with the tide and the net was beginning to fold on itself again. He moved to the wheelhouse and adjusted his course. As he turned his head to see his line up, his harpoon drove through his chest and stuck him to the electrically sparking console. In shock, he stared out through wide eyes and pointed before he weakly grasped the harpoon and slumped over, coughing and spitting up blood. In the moonlight, a figure of a woman stood in defiance on the stern rail, breathing heavily, bleeding from her eyes, ears and nose. Trails of blood from nail holes and ball bearing punctures trickled down her body. The captain and the woman watched as the creature in the net began to struggle again, swinging the net. The woman chopped the net line free from the boat and it vanished under water. The other side of the net was still attached to the tree. With the boat no longer tethered to the shore it headed out to sea. The woman jumped on deck and picked up a stick of dynamite, cut the fuse short and approached the captain who continued to drool blood. He was fading. The woman grabbed the captain by his hair and forcefully tilted his head back, watching his eyes blink slowly. With the console still sparking and electrical smoke trailing out of the open wheelhouse, the woman lit the dynamite fuse, stuck it in the console, turned, and in three strides, jumped off the back of the boat. The boat moved out to sea for a moment before exploding in a fireball followed by a secondary fuel explosion. From the surface water, the woman watched the remainder of the boat burn to the water line and sink.

2

As the schooner pulled out of Waisai Harbor, West Papua, a wavy black-haired woman with a slender build beamed a white smile and grabbed a stool to face a group of divers on the top deck of a live-a-board dive boat. She began her introduction, "Good afternoon everybody and welcome to the Eolian. The name is Latin and means, carried by the wind. It usually refers to wind carrying rock or sand, like the formation and migration of sand dunes. In our case, the Eolian is carrying us. The Eolian is a thirty-year old wood schooner built in Bira, Sulawesi, by some very reputable boat builders. It was used for many years as a cargo vessel all over South East Asia and then bought by this dive company and converted into a live-a-board. My name is Kylie Hughes. I'm from Tasmania. I will be your expedition leader on this nineteen-day dive adventure. I have been diving for eight years in Borneo and all over Indonesia as an instructor and guide, and have done this trip in both directions numerous times over the past few years. Originally, I wanted to be a veterinarian and I still love animals, but after university, I just wasn't ready to start that kind of career without seeing the world and it brought me here and us together. Hooray for that, eh? And no, we don't have two heads in Tasmania, at least most of us don't. There are twelve crewmembers including our Captain, his first mate, two deckhands, a chef and his apprentice, two experienced skiff drivers, and four dive guides. All the dive guides have underwater cameras for documenting our trip and the net removal process that you have all graciously paid for and volunteered your help. Making a difference is something to be proud of. There are ten guests so space is precious and so is fresh water. Let me start with a quick layout of the boat you'll be living on for the next few weeks. This area is the upper deck where we will be meeting for all meals, dive briefings, and any emergency. If you hear the bell, it's either time for a dive briefing or a meal. In case of an emergency, you will hear the bell ring ten times, pause, and ten more bells and so on. If you hear ten bells, drop what you are doing and get here as quick as possible without anything but yourselves. There are two recently inspected emergency raft canisters outside the port and starboard rails as you can see." Kylie pointed out at two opposing white canisters. "We will have a few emergency drills throughout the trip to be on the safer side of efficiency. We also have the two skiffs that we use to get to and from dive sites but can also be used in case of an emergency." Kylie pointed inside the port rail to a fastened table, "There is black tea, Nescafe, Milo, and packets of electrolytes with two hot and cold water dispensers available. In one refrigerator next to the water dispenser are juices and milk for you and some free space for your water bottles or whatever. You should all have a water bottle with your name on it to keep, reuse, and reduce your plastic footprint. I cannot emphasize enough how important it is to stay hydrated. Drinking eight bottles of water per day is not unheard of. Drinking water will alleviate muscle cramps, usually in your legs, and headaches during and after diving. If you misplace your bottle or leave it out, it will be collected and put in this box here below the honor sheet." She took a clipboard off the end of the table and held it up, "In the other refrigerator is beer and soft drinks for purchase. Be honest and put a tick along your name under either the soda category or the beer category. When we reach our final destination you can settle up in the office if you don't have cash on board. Don't worry about that now, you are here for a good time, you're going to see some amazing marine life, have an unforgettable experience, and clean up the discarded nets we find. Please remember for everyone's safety, if you are drinking beer or something harder, you need to stop drinking at least eight hours prior to diving. If we smell alcohol on you in the morning, you will have to wait out the first and maybe second dive. It's up to you, you paid for the expedition, but we have the final say on everybody's safety. You can sleep up here on the benches or out on the sun deck at night if you choose, but beware of periodic rain showers. Mind your electronics. This boat is on solar and generator power and is not the best for recharging, so don't leave your computers and such plugged in due to power surges. In the middle of the night, if you fall overboard while underway, we might not hear you and we would lose you to the current. If you're lucky, you'll play out the rest of your adventure in a Robinson Crusoe sequel. The masts are climbable during daylight hours but only when the engine is off and at anchor or on a mooring line. Please tell a crew member or a dive guide before you climb up. Underneath us are the reserved cabins for couples or whoever paid for a bigger state room. At the stern of the vessel on the same floor are two bathrooms with hot and cold fresh water showers and toilets with toilet paper and bum guns. Do not put anything in the toilet that you haven't eaten first. Use the bins provided for toilet paper, no matter what you do with it. Anything that goes in the toilet goes into the ocean and I don't want to see a bunch of toilet paper floating around while at a safety stop or surfacing from a dive. That goes with the shampoo and soap on the boat as well. We have biodegradable soap, shampoo, and conditioner, so leave your pricey soaps, shampoos and conditioners in your luggage. Your pricey products are mostly palm oil anyway. Palm oil is the bane of conservation and the world pays the high cost of deforestation of indigenous forests and gravely reduces animal habitat around the equatorial band. This dive company and most others refuse to support the palm oil industry. We hope you understand and support our position. We don't want your soaps and stuff to enter the ocean and you don't want to do more damage to the sea while you are here. If you have a question, please introduce yourself first."

A woman with brown hair and blue eyes asked in an American accent, "Hi, I'm Robyn Hines. This may be a stupid question but, what's a bum gun?"

People smiled and looked sheepishly around at the brunette American woman.

Kylie smiled at her and explained, "I'm glad you brought that up, Robyn. It's a nickname. A bum gun is for cleaning your privates, aka your bum, after going poop or whatever. South East Asian countries don't waste toilet paper like the west, but use water out of a bucket or a bum gun with a bit of pressure to do what toilet paper does without tearing down a forest to do it. Our bum guns and toilets are marine toilets so the water in them is saltwater. Please, if water is continuously running in a toilet, let one of the staff know. We don't want to burn out a pump motor or we'll be in a bit of a jam to fix it. There is a third bathroom under the stairs on the main deck, aft of the galley and the crew cabin. Please don't shower after every dive. Rinse off at the two showers on the back deck between your dives and save your soap shower for the end of the day. Please keep them short. We suggest what people call a military shower; get wet, turn off the water, lather up, shave and wash your hair, then rinse thoroughly and keep it short. The only place anybody can smoke cigarettes or vapes is outside on the aft main deck by the third bathroom closet. On both sides of the main deck are walkways to the front of the boat. The wheelhouse is where the captain and his mate drive the boat and have a sleeping bench behind, so please respect that area. Someone is usually asleep between shifts. The captain and mate both smoke so sometimes you can have a ciggy there, but don't crowd them. In front of the wheelhouse is our dive deck. Your gear should already be in crates with your names on them under the central countertop, or put it in if you still have it. Your tanks are along the side rails and benches. You will be reusing the same tank throughout this trip. Each time you come back from a dive, one of the crew will refill your tank without removing your gear. In front of the dive gear are two bins of fresh water. The one on the port side, left side, is for torches, masks and dive computers. The second bin is under the bench seat on the starboard side, right side, and is only used for cameras. They are both refilled with fresh water every time we go in for resupply, about every six days. An emergency oxygen bottle is strapped to the forward mast in case of a rescue emergency. In front of the mast is the bow, you can go there and have a look around. Sometimes you'll find a crew member sleeping there or searching for a phone signal from an island tower. You are free to use the area as they do. Below the wheelhouse and behind the galley is a set of stairs to the lower cabins. Most cabins are double occupancy except for the forward cabin which sleeps six. There are fire extinguishers in every room in the event of an electrical fire. There is no smoking of any kind in the cabins. In the wheelhouse on the port side is a small first aid kit for your simple needs. We have plenty more of everything so if you use up something like tape or motion sickness tablets and can't find any more, let one of us know and we will restock it for you. If you know you get seasick or are not sure, take a motion sickness pill right now and continue taking them. It will make your trip a lot more fun. There is a larger first aid kit in the cabinet also in the wheelhouse where it's relatively dry and centrally located. Most of you will be staying below deck. The only area we don't want you going is the two hatches all the way aft. One leads to the engine room and the other is where we stow the bagged rubbish and all abandon nets we collect off the reefs. The nets will be going ashore to be destroyed when we resupply. I will introduce the crew to you later but I have to ask a second time just in case something was amiss in the paperwork. Are there any vegetarians, vegans, people with food allergies, or people with special food restrictions or needs we should know about? The paperwork says no." Kylie looked over the group and no one raised their hand. "Great. I want to take the time to thank you all very much for volunteering your time to help us clean the reefs while on this unforgettable voyage. There are sets of knives and small wire cutters on slinky cords in each of your dive equipment crates. Please attach them to your buoyancy control device, also known as a BCD and do not unclip them or you may lose them and you are responsible for them."

The American girl, Robyn asked, "What does your chef cook?"

Kylie replied, "Everything except seafood. It's company policy not to eat fish since we prefer to see them alive underwater rather than on your plate. If live-a-boards in these waters bought fish from local sources, the locals would then begin fishing our dive sites and that would be counterproductive. We don't want to create the demand. Are there any more questions before we get to introductions with your name, your country, and a little about yourself if you want?"

Robyn spoke up, "I saw sails. Do we sail much?"

Kylie shook her head, "We sail, but not too much because it's not practical considering we have time constraints to get to restock destinations and dive sites. Between opposing strong currents and periodic storms, sailing would most likely double our time between sites. We will drop the sails periodically for sunset pictures or in front of an active volcano further down our intended course. If the engine quits, for whatever reason, we sail on and that will be an adventure you will definitely tell your family and friends when you get home." Kylie paused and looked out into the afternoon sun. "Are there any more questions?" Kylie looked around the group ending to her left and smiled, nodded, and raised her eyebrows at the man sitting next to her, "Would you please introduce yourself to the rest of us?"

"Hello. My name is Mark Tassley. I'm from San Francisco, California, and I'm really psyched to be out here diving in these remote waters while they're still relatively pristine." Mark looked to his left.

"Hi. I'm Isabela. I'm from Italy and here with my boyfriend, Zayne." Isabela put her hand on the bleach blond tattooed man's knee sitting next to her.

Zayne raised his hand and smiled, "Hello. I'm Zayne from South Africa. I live in Sweden with Isabela." He looked to his left as Isabela bent around Zayne to see who was going to speak next.

"Hello. My name is Caroline. I'm from England and finished my Instructor course in Labuan Bajo before this trip. All I have to add is, whatever you do, do it with passion." She looked to her left.

"How ya goin'? I'm Alec Bain from Australia. I've been surfing most of my life and decided to take the plunge a few years back, and that lead to a whole new addiction to the seas and oceans around the world."

"Ola. I am Raoul from Buenos Aires, Brazil. I have a Masters in Marine Biology. My hobby is photography in any environment. I also have a Tech Diving Certificate and I brought my gear hoping someone else has the same." Raoul looked around and saw no response from the others. He shrugged his shoulders.

"I'm Tom Wesley from Brixton, England and very excited about shedding this pasty white shell and seeing some amazing marine life."

"I'm Robyn Hines from California. I have an Architectural Engineering degree and just quit my job after six years to come out here and see how other people live and dive around the world."

"My name is Pierre Montague from Montpellier, France. I am a chef in Paris on a six-week holiday and then back to work. I am looking for an unforgettable experience to carry me through the next year of work in a hot and busy kitchen." Pierre looked to his left.

"Hello, my name Scott Bentley from San Diego, California. I've been diving in many places around the world and this is the last big spot on the bucket list. I also have a Tech Diving Cert. and a Dive Instructor Certificate, but I doubt they can mix gases on this trip." Scott looked at Raoul.

Raoul nodded in agreement in Scott's direction.

Isabela scoffed, "Oh come on, seriously, three people from California out of ten around the world."

Robyn responded calmly, "Actually, there aren't many Americans traveling these days because the U.S. news companies want us to believe the rest of the world is out to get us and, in some places, to kill us. I haven't met very many Americans travelling in the last six months until now. Have you, Isabela?"

"No, but three out of ten? That's a lot."

Robyn nodded and replied, "I agree with you and I know of our country's reputation. I hope you are pleasantly surprised."

Kylie stepped in. "Lovely. Now let me introduce you to your dive guides. There are three guides besides myself."

An Indonesian woman with jet-black wavy hair raised her hand and announced in broken English, "Welcome aboard the Eolian everybody, my name Sari, I'm living in Labuan Bajo. I become dive guide in Komodo and Labuan Bajo six years ago. I come up on the Eolian seven months ago to dive the sites in Raja Ampat and have been diving and working at a resort in Waisai and another in Misool. I am very familiar with these waters we are going to dive. Now we dive to my home and you will see what I know."

A slender man with bleach blonde hair and blue eyes stood up and waved, "Hello, I'm Chris, Kylie's partner. I've been trying to teach her English for a few years now and she's slowly getting it." People chuckled as Chris continued, "I was born in the landlocked part of the States but quickly realized I belonged in the sea. My father moved to California and I had the choice to either stay with my mother in Idaho or go with him to California. He got me into diving around the age of nine and I've been at it ever since. I never went to college and barely made it out of high school in Coronado, California. I spent all my time in the ocean, surfing, diving or playing volleyball on the beach. I began Navy SEAL training at my father's request and that was my path of least resistance. I have a Technical Dive Instructor Cert. and six years training with the SEALs. As they say, 'the easiest day was yesterday'. I'm sure we three Techs can get a couple of deep dives in at the right sites, current and weather dependent. There are also a lot of unexplored cave systems where we are going so we should have some good opportunities. But Scott is correct, we can't mix gases on this voyage."

"Hi, I'm Sophie Burns from England. I have been diving all over Thailand, Philippines, Myanmar, and Indonesia for about eight years as a dive guide and instructor with this company and others. I've been to most of the sites we are going to at least a couple times and want to say you are going to be diving in some very remote places that very few people have ever dived before. I studied South East Asian history at university and will be happy to try and answer any questions you have about the area or its people. I will also be offering short 'walk and talks' about the history of the areas as we pass through, the Dutch occupation of Indonesia, and other foreign conquerors that had a major influence exploring and exploiting the region. Other than that, let's go diving!"

Everybody applauded each other and brimmed with smiles and adventurous hoots.

Kylie pulled out a rough hand drawn expedition map showing the island chain and course the Eolian was going to take from Raja Ampat to Komodo Island. She pointed to a number 'one' on the map. "Right. So here we are in Raja Ampat leaving Waisai, Waigeo. Waigeo Island is the largest island of the four main islands. Raja Ampat translates to four kings. The other three main islands are Salawati, Batanta, and Misool. We are heading for our first dive this afternoon primarily to make sure your gear is in working order, weighted properly, and give you time to familiarize yourself with your gear and your buoyancy. This will all come into play for every dive. It's important to get your gear right so the rest of the dives are hassle free. I know many of you brought underwater cameras, but please do not take them on this first dive. I want you all to focus on your gear and make any adjustments necessary and not be distracted by taking pictures of fish, sharks, or colorful coral. You will have plenty of time for that as we carry on. Your dive groups are listed here at the bottom, and they may change. Your guides will find you and introduce themselves and meet you at your dive gear soon. Just enjoy the dive. In about two hours, one of the guides will get in a skiff and go check what the current is doing, and then the bell will sound for the dive briefing. We meet here and one of the guides will brief you all on the site, the current, what you may expect to see, and your depth and time limits. I'm sure you all know this but I have to mention it, please do not drink any alcoholic beverages until after your last dive of the day. Enjoy the afternoon and see you in a few hours. Oh, and there will be some fruit and snacks set out here for you shortly. We will do our check dive and dinner will be served underway around 7 pm. We will make way throughout the night and arrive at our next dive site sometime in the middle of the night." Kylie pointed at her map at a site with the number 'two' next to it. We will dive in this area for four dives with a night dive as the forth dive before we move on. I cannot guarantee any certain number of dives but we usually dive around fifty-five dives during the expedition. Thank you for your time and let the adventure begin."

People clapped and began to stir, getting up and moving about the boat. Some went off to find their dive gear and make sure everything was there, others returned to their cabins to unpack, and a few moved to the sun deck to take in the view and shoot photos. Mark got up and crossed the deck to the cups hanging over the water dispensers and fixed himself a tea.

Robyn walked up behind him, grabbed an electrolyte powder packet, poured it into her water bottle and filled it up with cold water at the second dispenser. She looked at Mark and spoke, "So, San Francisco, huh?"

Mark looked over and replied, "Yep, most of my life."

"In the city or just a reference point?"

"Marin County boy."

Robyn nodded and replied, "Thought so. I went to Cal Poly, San Luis Obispo first then transferred to Berkeley."

"A California girl born and bred," said Mark with a smirk and continued, "How long are you traveling for?"

Robyn shrugged and answered, "Yes to your first point, and as to your question, as long as the money holds out and I have some left to start over again somewhere." She pulled her water bottle away from the dispenser and looked at Mark and added, "Again."

"Oh?" Mark asked, "Do you travel a lot or is it due to work or what?"

"It started in college, heading to Mexico with friends. After Berkeley I took most of my stuff home to my folk's house and put it in their basement. When I got to Berkeley, I had nothing but a mountain bike and a backpack. I left the same way except for an additional big bag of debt. I signed up with a company until my debts were paid then I saved some money to get out. I really don't have a plan. You?"

Mark stirred his tea and moved to an open table and sat down with Robyn following him. Mark replied, "I got a worthless degree and worked at everything from waiting tables, bike courier, carpentry, lifeguard, deckhand, all kinds of things but nothing really drew me in as a career. Nothing I woke up to excited me except payday." Mark smiled weakly.

Robyn asked, "So do you think all travelers are 'lost-causes' looking for connections?"

Mark nodded, "In my case, probably. I think travel is one of the tools of experience and through it, you may learn what you don't want to do in life as well as maybe find something that inspires you like Kylie did. One minute she's going to be a vet and the next, she's out here doing something that she loves to do, travel, scuba dive, conservation, make a difference and a little money at the same time. Nobody gets rich being a dive guide, it's a way of life. Maybe it's that pause that allows us to make better decisions."

Robyn asked, "Are you traveling alone?"

"Yep. You?"

Robyn nodded and explained, "Yeah. I was in a relationship but we grew apart and I wasn't ready to get married and settle down. He was getting pushy and adding pressure to an already anxious situation. I wanted more out of my life and he liked his job. There's no time like the present to get on with it."

"Indeed." Mark continued, "I don't want to do it all after retirement when I can't enjoy the outdoors like I should or a mishap occurs and I lose the ability to fulfill some dreams. Do you know what dive group you're in?"

"Ah, yeah, I'm diving with Kylie, Raoul, and the Aussie guy."

"Alec."

"Yeah, him. How about you?"

"He's diving with me," answered Chris, walking over to shake hands with Mark and then with Robyn. He sat down next to Robyn, looking at Mark and continued, "Our group is you, Pierre and Caroline. Our gear is forward on the port side." Chris pointed to the left side of the boat. "We arranged the groups by experience level but they can change due to Tech divers wanting to dive together, illness, compatibility, but this is how we start and then modify as needed. Your group, Mark, all have an Advanced Certification and Rescue certs and all have over five hundred dives so we grouped you together expecting you all to have about the same experience level and air consumption. Excuse me a minute." Chris got up to help the cook and the staff carry up snacks to a long table. They placed assorted dishes of fruit, cakes and vegetable plates for everyone, then the bell sounded outside the wheelhouse. People getting organized in their rooms came up and those relaxing on the sundeck sat up and began to move. A small line of people formed at the stack of plates and began the first buffet of many.

Robyn and Mark didn't move, they just waited for the line to run through as Robyn asked, "Who are you rooming with?"

"Tom, the guy from England. And you?"

"Caroline. She seems nice. I think she's really excited to be on this adventure."

Chris returned and interjected, "Aren't you, Robyn?"

"Yes, of course, but some people show it on the outside more than others and she seems easy to read."

Chris elaborated, "Emotional and sensitive type you think?"

Robyn said, "She used the term 'passionate'. That's probably what I'm picking up on, but I'm not here to profile anyone. Excuse me, I'm getting in line."

Mark watched Robyn as she got up and grabbed a plate and selected some papaya, mango, watermelon and fried bananas. Her body was that of an athlete, flat stomach and muscular tone to her arms and legs. She turned around and noticed Mark looking at her. She didn't mind. She returned to Mark's table and suggested, "You should grab some fruit before the good stuff disappears."

"Right." Mark slid out from his seat and headed to the plates. The tables filled up with people chatting and getting acquainted. Mark could overhear most of the conversations in English. The only two that weren't speaking English were Zayne and Isabela who sat together chatting away in Swedish.

Mark returned to his table and was joined by Pierre. Chris and the other staff went to the buffet after the guests had all had a turn. Pierre reached out his hand to Mark, "Hello, I'm Pierre. Nice to meet you."

Mark smiled and greeted Pierre, "Yeah, you too. I'm Mark. I think we are diving together."

Pierre reiterated, "Yeah, Chris said you, me and Caroline dive together. So how many dives do you have and where?"

Mark replied modestly, "Many all over the place."

Pierre's eyes opened wide. "Oh, was good?"

Mark smiled, "Yeah, good." He knew Pierre wanted him to ask how many dives he has so he didn't.

Pierre nodded and looked at Robyn, "And you? How many dives do you have?"

"Oh, I have a couple hundred, many within the last six months. I was diving off Koh Tao, Thailand and got my Open Water and Advanced, back to back. I didn't feel comfortable diving just eight or ten times in the ocean and a few in the pool. I wasn't ready to go dive everywhere without more experience, so I kept after it and dived the Similan Islands, Koh Lanta, Koh Phi Phi, and Koh Lipe in Thailand, Tioman Island in Malaysia and some other places." Robyn looked at Pierre who was nodding while eating.

Mark just smiled and asked Robyn, "What did you think of Koh Phi Phi?"

Robyn put her fork down and sat up straight, "It was a mess! They are building themselves out of paradise and going straight up. When you go diving, there are boats coming from Phi Phi, Phuket, Krabi, Ao Nang and everybody is running over each other. The dive sites are crowded and the water boils with bubbles. The thing that really got me frustrated was that I couldn't go to some beaches in the smaller island coves without paying a lot of money. After seeing all the tourists, I wouldn't go back anyway. Phi Phi was a frat-boy party at night and not really my style."

Pierre agreed, "I think same. Too much busy people and a lot of it is run by some unsavory types who think the rules don't apply to them. I also heard that two Russians died after being run over by a speed boat some years ago. Pas bon." He shook his head.

Mark tried to turn the conversation, "I'm glad we are way out here where most people can't reach yet. We should have the dive sites to ourselves for the most part."

Kylie walked up behind Robyn, "Robyn, hi, how was the fruit?"

Robyn nodded. "Good, really sweet."

"Good to hear. Listen, when you're all finished here would you meet me up front and we'll locate your gear crate and make sure everything fits okay before we jump in the water?" Kylie moved toward the stairs.

Robyn said, "Sure, I'm done. Where do I put my plate?"

Kylie looked around at everybody's plates, silverware and cups and spoke quietly to Robyn, "Thank you. That reminds me. Excuse me a minute everybody." Kylie moved to the middle of the upper deck and announced, "I forgot to mention? Just there, next to the refrigerators, are three garbage bins, one for compost waste, one for recycling beer, soda cans, glass and plastic bottles, and the third is for general waste that doesn't belong in the other two bins. Your plates, cups and silverware go in the black tub. Okay? I'd like to meet with my dive group, Robyn, Raoul and Alec up front in five-ten minutes. Okay, see you there."

Isabela walked up to Kylie with her phone in her hand and asked, "Is there an internet connection? I have 4G but can't find a signal."

Kylie smiled at her and apologized, "Sorry darling, internet connections are spotty at best along the way but you will have connection when we pull into a harbor to resupply and throw away nets. We will be in those resupply harbors for at least twenty-four hours each. If you see a tower along the way you should have service."

Isabela had an unsettled look on her face as Kylie walked off down the stairs.

After overhearing Isabela, Robyn got up and rolled her eyes at Mark, "Chat at ya later." She put her plate in the black tub, went downstairs past the wheelhouse, and disappeared forward.

3

FIVE DAYS LATER

It was before dawn when Mark walked up the stairs past the wheelhouse to the upper deck where he found many guests and crew members sleeping on the benches and on the sundeck. He grabbed a languidly swinging cup from a hook and placed it on the bench between the two water dispensers. He opened a jar of tea bags and put one in his cup and then added hot water. Opening the refrigerator, he fumbled around for the milk and poured some in his cup along with a spoonful of sugar. His day had begun. He looked out into the sunrise and saw the silhouette of a string of islands in the distance. It was their next dive site. Mark sat on the stairs above the wheelhouse watching the sea.

Robyn walked up the stairs to get a coffee. "Good morning."

Mark replied, "Good morning. Sleep well?"

As Robyn stepped up past Mark, she mumbled, "Caroline snores like a man."

Mark chuckled.

When she returned with a coffee, she sat behind Mark on a stair above and enjoyed the view and the quiet.

The sun crept up the horizon, changing the colors of the sky with swaths of red, orange and yellow. Pink illuminant trim edged approaching Cumulus clouds and reflected across the calm sea surface. The Eolian chugged through a glassy ground swell. Stars disappeared in the oncoming light.

Robyn looked down at Mark's back and asked quietly, "I know we still have two weeks of diving left, but I was curious what your plans are afterward?"

Mark turned his head up and sideways, "I haven't gotten that far yet. I was thinking of diving Komodo for a few days until I heard they raised the day visitor fees beyond my financial reach. I've also been thinking of making my way back toward Bali or Lembongan by boat. I don't really know. I also hear a lot about how amazing the diving is around Pulau Weh, on the Andaman Sea."

Robyn nodded while watching flying fish leap out of the wake and glide to safety. "So, I've known you for five days now and all we ever talk about is diving and underwater photos. Can I be blunt and ask, what's your story? You're traveling alone and haven't spoken of a wife, girlfriend or significant other left behind or pining away for your devoted return."

Mark again looked over his shoulder at Robyn, "Why do you ask?"

"I don't know. You seem like a nice guy. Just wondering why you're single I guess. Maybe I want an interview, who knows." Robyn smiled.

Mark smiled and stated, "An interview, huh? You are blunt. I like that. So I'll be honest back." Mark paused and took a deep breath before he explained, "I lost my fiancé, Tira, in a car accident a few years back. We met as dive buddies on Koh Tao and traveled and dived South East Asia together ending up in Labuan Bajo, Flores. We worked for a dive shop, doing day trips around Komodo and Rinca Islands. When the dive season ended, we returned to the U.S. to make money with intensions of returning to South East Asia. We were both mesmerized by the beauty of the sea and the different languages and cultures. We were living that dream lifestyle that is so hard to find." Mark took a sip of his tea and continued, "When I was boxing up Tira's personal belongings, I found her journal. I had respectfully never read it." Mark sighed. "But before packing it away, I sat down and read it. I felt guilty for doing so, but it also brought me closer to her. I learned more about her family than I wanted to know and I learned more about her than I could have ever fathomed. The things that went through her head like breaking away from city life and focusing on rescuing the oceans were important to her. There were addresses, phone numbers, websites, volunteer programs, all listed as the last entry. I jotted down the information and researched it to see where she was headed, where we were headed. We weren't city dwellers and she was edging out when the car accident occurred. I decided to follow one of her dreams because the city now only reminded me of Tira and the only place I thought I was going to be truly happy again was under thirty meters of water in a screaming current."

"I'm sorry for your loss. I didn't expect that answer." Robyn defused the sadness. "I just figured you were an accountant." Robyn smiled.

Mark laughed. "An accountant. That exciting, huh? It's all right. It feels good to talk about it to the right people. My shrink told me it would help me heal and move on."

Robyn put a hand on Mark's shoulder and said, "Well, you can talk to me if you want. But not about the square root of Pi or anything over my head. Were you back in California when it happened?"

"Yeah. I was making good money but let go due to the Corona Virus pandemic. I struggled through and fought with vaccines and depression like so many others. Time passed and I came to the realization that life was too short to be caught up in the rat race for the rest of my life. With Tira gone, something had to change and I had to make it happen. I decided on one of the more adventurous of Tira's options. After I saved up a bunch of money, I hopscotched from San Francisco to Inchon, South Korea, Bangkok, Krabi, Bali, Makassar, Sarong, and ferried to Waisai Harbor where we all got on this boat five or six days ago."

Kylie climbed the stairs past Mark and Robyn. Without saying anything Kylie gave Mark and Robyn a nod and a sleepy smile as she went up for a Nescafé.

Mark realized this expedition was a truly monumental feat for anybody and it had just begun.

The skipper sat at the wheel in a tall swivel chair driving with his feet and periodically getting up to look out about the bow for floating debris, logs or oncoming vessels. There was little traffic. Mark noticed the boat had radar and an automated identification system (AIS), but it was turned off.

As the morning approached, the captain throttled down to a drift as the Eolian shallowed up toward an atoll. The skipper told two deckhands to man the anchor wench and prepare for release. The captain looked over the side of the boat waiting for a sandy place to drop the anchor. One of the skiffs came alongside and Kylie jumped in and sped off toward the first designated morning dive site. Most of the guests were up with coffee or tea watching as the skiff cruised along a cliff where the current was boiling in swirls. Everybody was hypnotized by the beauty and clarity of the sea. Chris answered the handheld radio and wrote down the information from Kylie. The sky was clear above and the sun climbed through the blue from the East. The captain ordered the deckhands to drop anchor.

"Roger that. Eolian out." Chris put the radio back in its recharging holder and walked behind the captain and rang the bell.

Those that were up already grabbed a light snack and sat down, chatting about the beauty of the islands, shooting pictures, again giddy with excitement of the dives and the day to come. Some sleepyheads climbed the stairs and headed for the coffee and tea.

Once everyone had arrived, whether they were seated or getting coffee, Chris held up a hand-drawn placard of the dive site and began, "Good morning everyone. Welcome to the Forgotten Islands. I hope you slept well. We have three incredible dives for you today with thirty-five-meter visibility and the water temperature is holding at 27 C. We know there are nets here, so keep your eyes peeled. Two dive groups will be diving along this cliff here and the other two will be diving along the atoll slope." Chris pointed out to the island cliff across from the atoll. "Kylie spotted a big net attached to that little tree on the atoll and it is draped into the deep, caught on coral and rock. It's pinned to the channel floor and looks like it crosses over. We are going to send a couple deckhands to the island to connect the line off the tree to a skiff when the time

comes. The primary underwater work will be my group and
Kylie's on the first dive. The goal, as always, is to free the net
without breaking the coral and drag the net or buoy it to a
skiff and load it in the hold with the others. There can be
strong currents here but since the current is just changing, we
have some time before it begins to rage. Along the cliff, your
dive guide will keep you in or near the little coves along the
way. You want to hold up and definitely look for small stuff
clinging to the wall. As usual, follow your guide. Watch your
dive computer. It's important since we've had at least three
dives per day. As you know, how deep you dive on the first
dive affects your second and third dive as it relates to
decompression. If you go into deco, you will miss all the dives
in the next twenty-four hours or maybe more. And that, my
friends, simply will not do. Okay, enough of the lecture and
back to the description of the dive site. When you are in these
small coves don't forget to look out into the blue for
hammerheads, whitetips, blacktip sharks, whale sharks,
dolphins, tuna, turtles, marble rays, devil rays, eagle rays,
manta rays, pilot whales, all kinds of big stuff. Every dive is
different. This is our first dive of the day so the maximum
depth is thirty meters. At seventy bar, tell your guide so your
group can comfortably start your accent to your safety stop.
The other two groups can chill out and wait for us to get in the
skiffs, then come down and suit up. Are there any questions?"
Chris looked around and nobody moved. "Good. Let's get wet."

Kylie had returned and met her group on the starboard
side of the dive deck to get ready. Chris let Caroline go first
down the port side and then lit a cigarette at the edge of the
wheelhouse knowing she would take some time to get into
her wetsuit. Mark and Pierre sat with Chris for a moment

before heading down to get ready. Pierre donned his wetsuit easily and Mark didn't wear one. They were ready in a minute while Caroline struggled with plastic bags on her feet to help get through her wetsuit leggings.

The skiffs were in place. Kylie turned on her air, shouldered her BCD and tank, grabbed her mask and fins, and hopped in the skiff followed slowly by her group. The skiff pulled away heading for the cliffside of the dive site. Mark pulled all the rest of Caroline's gear out of the crate and set it close to the edge. Finding the biodegradable liquid soap, he put drops in his, Caroline's, and Pierre's masks. Chris finished his smoke and put on his gear in seconds trying to hold Mark and Pierre back from getting on the skiff without Caroline. After wrestling with her suit, she put her BCD and tank on and Mark and Caroline buddy-checked each other's gear before heading to the skiff. Caroline knew she was the slowest of the group and gently turned Mark around to face the skiff and gave him a nudge, "Let's go."

Chris directed the skiff near the weathered tree on the atoll.

The divers were ready and Chris counted, "On three. One, two, three, drop."

The four divers back rolled into the sea and returned to the surface briefly. The skiff cleared away from the divers and sped off toward the Eolian for the next group. Chris turned a thumb down and everybody submerged breathing out slightly and releasing air from their BCD. The current moved everybody along the shallows toward the edge of deeper water. Across the narrow channel, Kylie's dive group left bubble trails as they descended, combing the wall for marine life and discarded nets. Mark spied a school of barracuda circling in a cone as he drifted down with the current. Chris pointed to the sea floor and put his hand on top of his head like a shark fin. Mark looked down and saw a whitetip shark swimming languidly against the growing current. Mark searched for the others and found Caroline near the wall watching large fish swim past and feed on clouds of small glassfish. Pierre remained a few meters above Chris playing with his GoPro settings. Chris arrived at twenty-five meters and signed to the other three divers, "Okay?"

Everybody responded with the okay sign.

Chris drifted ahead and began making hand signals for what marine life he passed, then he saw the net below and pointed to it. The net line crossed the shallow reef and sagged toward the sheer cliff below Kylie's group.

Chris rounded everybody up and pulled out a white square board and began writing on it. When he turned the board around, it showed their positions along the net. Caroline would start in the shallows and work toward Pierre, then Pierre would cut the net free toward Chris. Chris at the deepest point would work toward Mark at the far end of the net.

Mark pointed to the snarled net on the opposing rock face, and Chris gave him the okay sign. Mark swam toward the snag, frog kicking diagonally into the growing current toward the cliffside. Pierre and Chris went to their positions along the net. Chris noticed Kylie's group had stopped in the ravines and had abruptly turned back to ascend slowly toward where they had jumped in, but at a shallower depth, looking for different marine life and not engaging in the net removal due to the growing current and their experience level.

When Mark got to his position he took a moment to observe the others begin cutting the net free from the rocks. As he began freeing the net, he noticed all the hooks in the mesh had been bent straight. Mark was pushed by an unseen surge of water and spontaneously ripped from his position. Caught in a downcurrent, he immediately inflated his BCD and kicked frantically toward the cliff. He flashed a glance over at the rest of the team and saw them in an upcurrent kicking downward and letting air out of their BCDs. His group watched and pointed at Mark as he helplessly tumbled over the cliff drawn into the abyss and out of sight.

Chris noticed Mark's bubbles weren't leaving a trail to the surface, meaning the current was continuing to take him and his bubbles downward. Pierre and Caroline looked at each other, at their gauges, then continued searching for signs of Mark. As the current got stronger with no signs of Mark, Chris crossed his arms aborting the dive. They all continued hanging on the net cable and shallowed up, hand over hand, to their safety stop. Chris aborted the safety stop and they all followed him into the shallows where they could take off their fins and stand. All three of them whistled, yelled and waved their arms to get the attention of one of the skiffs dropping off a second group along the cliff.

The current continued to draw Mark down with his BCD fully inflated. He slowed and noticed swimming shadows below him too dark to identify. He grabbed at a rock face and heard dolphins clicking and sounding, as one came close and nudged him. Mark knew the current would be weakest along the wall but fear gripped him as the current continued to twist and suck him downward. His legs flailed while trying to maintain a purchase on the rock face. He lost his grip and

37

plummeted deeper into nothing. Out of the blue, a dolphin pushed Mark toward the rock wall with the current pressing steadily. He lunged for the rock and set a reef hook attached to his BCD jacket to hold him in place. He looked at his computer. One hundred meters. He looked at his air gauge, 100 bar, half-tank. He realized he was already in decompression trouble and would need help from shipmates on the surface if he wanted to reach it. Mark could just see the bottom of the net and began to climb hoping other divers would show up with tanks or he'd have to exhale to the surface and succumb to decompression sickness and possibly death. He looked up the rock wall tapering off to a slope to his right. Thinking of staying in the lee side of the current, Mark latched on to the base of a coral and moved out of the stronger current. As he climbed hand over hand, resetting his reef hook as he went, he saw a large animal above him entangled in the net. As he approached, Mark took the time to cut the beast loose. It was the biggest, fattest eel he had ever seen. The animal swam off. Desperately, but calmly, Mark continued climbing the ridge knowing his oxygen level was going down with every breath. He considered taking air from his BCD valve knowing the air would expand as he ascended. He knew the air bubbles would begin to emerge from the BCD valve at capacity as the air expanded. He could see the distant pale blue light of the surface.

Fifteen minutes had passed on the surface with Kylie aborting the dive and frantically reviewing the search and rescue protocols and alternative procedures beginning with the two skiffs and spotters doing a surface grid search. Chris organized an underwater search to follow the current down to extract Mark. Raoul, one of the other technical divers, got busy setting up his gear with extra tanks and a static line to follow Mark's path into the deep and return.

Robyn noticed dolphins surfacing and jumping around the boat.

As Mark climbed the ridge, dolphins repeatedly swam close. He reached a rock outcrop at the edge of a deep dark crevasse cut into the cliff. Looking up on the opposite wall of the crevasse, he saw a blue-green light reflecting off a sandy recess. The eel he had freed swam past him into the crevasse. Mark watched a dolphin disrupt a surface reflection and swiftly return to him. Mark realized the dolphins were getting air in the ravine light. He couldn't make it to the surface so he began to make his way toward the light and into a naturally lit cave. He looked at his dive computer showing 80 meters. His air gauge read 60 bar. Mark surfaced in the cave. The sandy bottom broke the surface water onto a miniature half-moon sandbank with two dark recesses. He pulled his mouthpiece out cautiously and took a successful breath. He took off his mask and fins and stood amazed at all the phosphorescent algae on the walls of the cave. He walked out of the water and onto a warm mound of sand where he took off his BCD and tank, and dropped his weight belt. The eel swam languidly back and forth watching him from the shallows like a dog waiting to go for a walk. A dolphin bobbed for air. Mark's eyes met one of the dolphin's eyes and then the eye of the eel like beast. The dolphin chattered loudly echoing through an unseen labyrinth of chambers. Mark went to his kit, turned off his air tank, grabbed his surface marker buoy and walked back in the water blowing air into the tube and unwinding his spool. He took a deep breath and swam down the cave ceiling to the opening and let the SMB loose to rise to the surface or as high as possible. Mark swam back into the cave. His buoy line spun rapidly to the end but the surface marker buoy didn't reach the surface. He grabbed the spool and untangled the last few coils. The line remained taut. He could feel the surge of the sea in the line. He clipped the line to his BCD and sat in the sand exhausted. In the cave shallows, the beast quietly raised its head above the water line. Mark had never seen anything like it. It had four legs and the body of a giant eel. Mark stood up and turned to survey his surroundings. Camouflaged by rock and green-blue phosphorescent glow, two dark eyes appeared. As Mark drew near, the eyes closed and blended into the wall. Mark looked where the eyes were and saw nothing. He turned and kept looking around the cave. The eyes opened again, watching Mark's back. The beast splashed in the water and Mark went to it and crouched down. The beast came closer with its mouth open.

Startled, Mark pushed backward, crab crawling away from the water's edge. The beast stopped. Mark saw three large stainless steel hooks in the beast's mouth, identical to those straightened on the net above. He got up and retrieved his snips and showed them to the animal.

The beast opened its mouth wider showing rows of teeth and moved into the shallows. Mark reached in and cut the barbs off the hooks and backed the stems out. Mark finished and moved back away from the edge of the water and looked at the animal.

The animal blinked, its eyes calmly staring at Mark.

Mark said, "I'll take that as a thank you."

Another dolphin surfaced and looked at him. Two more dolphins had entered the shallows. The beast sat very still, looking off toward the back wall.

Mark looked at the beast's iridescent neck scales, dark ear holes, and its bulbous forehead. "What are you?"

A woman peeled away from the wall, pointing a sword at Mark's neck and said frankly, "It's a baby sea dragon."

Startled by a voice, Mark fell backward, bracing himself with his arms and legs half in the water. "What the ...!" He looked up at a woman as her skin changed color like a chameleon.

Threatened, she asked, "What are you doing here? How did you get here?"

Mark shook his head and didn't know what to say.

"Answer me or I'm going to kill you!"

Mark put his hands up and explained, "We were diving and clearing nets above here and I got caught in a downcurrent."

The woman eyed Mark and responded, "You really shouldn't dive alone."

"I wasn't. I was diving with three others and they got caught in an upcurrent. It all happened so fast. I was only a little way away from them, maybe twenty-thirty meters when the current forced me down."

The woman nodded at the beast and it went out of the cave.

"Where's it going?"

"He's going to go have a look around." She put her sword in its sheath. As the woman moved, her skin went tan. She wore a silk sarong over one shoulder loosely covering her body to her knees. Her sun-bleached hair fell over her shoulders. "He's also known as a water dragon by local legends. He was a gift from my father long ago. I think it was a gift to protect me from the outside world, or at least that is what he is growing into. But you changed that by helping him and he decided to save your life instead of eat you." She smiled. Her blue eyes glowed like the luminescent walls. "Come out of the water, but wash your hands first."

Mark was stunned and asked, "Wash my hands?"

She pointed after the sea dragon and explained, "He's got the bite of a Komodo dragon, it's a fatal infection within seven days and the saliva causes paralysis and sleep for long periods of time, long enough for the dragon to eat you alive."

Mark used the wet sand to help wash his hands and asked, "Who are you?"

"That depends."

"On what?"

"Your education most likely. I've gone by many names." She moved to a small waterfall and poured two glasses of water and handed one to Mark.

Mark reached for the glass.

She moved her fingers to touch over his and said, "I'm a rather private person and you are an uninvited guest in my house."

Mark apologetically responded, "I apologize for the intrusion. It was unintended. There will be a search and rescue for sure and I'll be out of here in no-time."

"We don't like intruders, not even cute ones. And you should never have gotten this deep. It's never happened before. Most divers die or get eaten by the sea dragon." She put her glass down. "Come on, I don't eat people. I kill people but I don't eat them." She watched Mark's eyes and expression.

In Mark's bewilderment he shook his head in confusion and asked, "Why am I not dead already?"

Again she looked into Mark's eyes and nodded at the water, "Dead? Did the sea dragon and the dolphins not save you by coaxing you here? If they hadn't, you'd certainly be dead. And as coincidence has it, I have no need for you dead."

"That's not what I meant. Even with the animals saving me, without a compression chamber, my blood should be boiling. Wait. What?"

"Oh that." She walked toward a pair of rock-wall sculpted chairs and sat down in the larger of the two, "What does your time piece tell you?"

"My time piece? Oh." Mark looked at his dive computer on his wrist, "My dive computer says I'm at 74 meters but I'm," he looked puzzled and continued, "no longer diving."

"Ah, computer, that's the word. The entrance to this room is at 80 meters and you are now in a natural decompression chamber. Due to the volcanic activity below us, it heats and pressurizes the trapped air in pockets throughout the labyrinth, making this place one large compression chamber. While you are here, the tide will breathe in and out, pressure will ease, and you will be shallowing up enough to walk out of here. But it's not today and maybe not tomorrow. Tell me, how long has your dive been?"

Mark looked at his computer, "70 minutes. My god, I need to get back to the surface."

The woman nodded slowly, understanding his desire and replied, "If you go now, you'll be dead on arrival."

Mark shook his head in question, "There is no way to quicken the rate of ascent. That's not possible, naturally."

"The volcanic magma is somewhat tidal, always liquid and fluid. It's synchronized with the gravity of the Moon and Sun, like the sea tides but slower. I can't exactly speed it up or slow it down. Please. Sit, relax, let's think." She offered the chair next to her with an open hand.

Mark moved and sat down.

The woman asked, "What do people call you?"

"Mark, my name is Mark."

"Mark? Mark what?"

"Mark Tassley."

"It's nice to meet you Mark Tassley. You're from America?"

"Yep."

"You can call me, Eirene. Tell me Mark, you came up from what, 100 meters to here?"

Mark nodded. "Yes. Something like that."

"Then you will be here at least twenty-four hours before you can venture to the surface or you can die trying. A few people, over the years, have tried and failed." Eirene watched Mark's eyes and body language as the information sank in. "I would like you to be my guest here and enjoy all I have to offer while equalizing."

Mark got up and paced nervously. "They are going to think I'm dead."

Eirene nodded and responded, "Hopefully."

Mark was confused as to why so long and questioned, "But you can get me to the surface in twenty-four hours?"

Eirene tilted her head in reluctant confirmation and offered, "That depends on you."

Mark felt drugged and weak and asked, "How do you figure?"

"As I said, Mark, if you exit the way you came in, you'll die. Tell me something about yourself. I don't see any jewelry on you, not even an earring."

"I don't like jewelry on me."

"So let me cut to the chase. Are you married?"

"No."

"Girlfriend?"

Mark nodded, "Working on it."

"Is she on the ship?"

"Yeah."

"But?"

"It's really not the right place. We talk a lot, but there's no privacy for that kind of intimacy. Too many people coming and going from rooms or dining area, that kind of thing. We've been talking about traveling together after the expedition. But then again, we're still trying to figure out how far we want to take it."

"But you like her?"

"Yes."

"How far are you willing to go to make it work?"

"When we get off the boat, we'll find out."

"So your relationship with this woman—is not consummated?"

"Consummated? No."

"What's her name?"

"Robyn."

"Well, if you want to see Robyn again, you're going to have to wait it out here."

"I don't really have a choice, do I?"

"No. Not if you want to live on the surface again. Keep an eye on your computer. It'll change in your favor even at this depth."

"I see." Mark looked down the hallway leading from the cave entrance and listened to water drops followed by faint echoes. There was a prolonged stillness. He knew Eirene was right about leaving through the cave. The decompression process was going to take time. "So, what happens now?" He checked his surface marker buoy holding the string and tugging. The marker was still taut. Eirene watched as Mark took off his black rash guard shirt and looked at his tan skin and fit body. Mark bent over to unzip his booties.

Eirene shrugged her shoulders, "Rest, eat, sleep, read a book and spend time with me, maybe I'll tell you a story or two. Come on, I'll show you around." Eirene got up and walked down a dark hallway. The algae on the walls began to glow around them as they moved through the passage and went dark after they passed. They rounded a bend and walked up to another level.

4

Once all divers were back on board the Eolian and Chris had explained everything to Kylie, she briefed the crew on company rescue protocols and placed her list of emergency numbers next to the satellite phone in the wheelhouse. She thought to wait and give herself and the crew the immediate opportunity to retrieve Mark or his body. Raoul and Chris inspected their dive gear together with extra air tanks. A deckhand tied tanks with regulators on lines at each end of the boat and dropped them every five meters to thirty meters. The other deckhand measured out two forty meter lines and two fifty meter lines and tied two tanks to each and lowered them into the water. Refilling the morning dive's partially used tanks had yet to be done.

Once the skiffs and divers were ready, Sophie and Sari jumped in one skiff and Raoul and Chris jumped in the second. Raoul mounted a small camera on top of his mask and turned it on before he and Chris tethered themselves to the skiff and back rolled into the sea. Chris followed the net ahead of Raoul. The current was a turbulent surge where Mark was last seen. There were still no bubbles. The beast swam up to Mark's surface buoy and chewed the line, releasing it to the surface. Chris and Raoul watched as the buoy limply rose up the cliff wall out of the deep. Chris and Raoul swam down watching their computers and sweeping their torch lights below. Their tether line spun on the skiff. Raoul watched a dark shadow move slowly back and forth below them hoping his camera was capturing the creature. Chris saw it also. Raoul looked for Mark's bubbles but saw nothing. They waited for a few minutes, searching their surroundings at 65 meters. Chris took off a spare tank and set it securely on a sand-covered rock shelf. Raoul did the same at a different location, just in case Mark missed one, he might find the other. There was nothing more they could do without getting decompression sickness themselves and headed back toward the surface to reconnect with the boat crew and report. Raoul put up his SMB to tell the skiff driver where they would approximately surface. Raoul and Chris did their safety stop and surfaced next to the skiff.

Raoul spit out his mouth piece and excitedly spoke to Chris, "Did you see that animal? What the hell was it!? You ever see one before? I hope I got clear footage. I've never seen anything like that before. Did you see it!?"

"Yeah, I saw it and I don't know what it is. But, you have to calm down. This isn't about a new species, this is about our friend, Mark. He's still down there. We need to get together with the others and figure this out in a hurry. Mark has no time left. He's going to run out of gas if he hasn't already. Chris grabbed the line draped over the edge of the skiff to remove his fins and got in the skiff. After Raoul got in he handed Chris Mark's surface marker buoy with a shred of line attached. Chris looked at the buoy and the line. It was frayed at the end and he showed Raoul concluding, "This looks like it was cut off on the rocks. We need to get back to the boat, now. Chris looked at the skiff driver and asked, "Can you take a GPS of this exact spot before moving. We left two tanks straight down here. Mark's close, below us and in trouble."

The skiff driver nodded, took the GPS coordinates before peeling out back to the Eolian to regroup. Raoul calmed down and looked at the footage on his camera of the beast. It wasn't as clear as he had hoped but he thought he could play with it on his computer when the time came.

Kylie used the Satellite phone in the wheelhouse to call the closest coast guard vessel and insurance numbers while the two skiffs continued searching the surface following the current. At the same time, guests lined the rails and watched for signs of Mark. Robyn was beside herself and insisted on climbing the main mast while the boat wasn't moving. She brought binoculars with her and peered out over the blue sea and on to the beaches and rock outcrops in case he had surfaced alive and made it to shore. She wasn't about to give up hope. She had grown very fond of Mark and was hoping for a more meaningful relationship than just dive buddies. He was a perfect match for her and completed her in ways she never expected from any man.

5

Eirene asked as she continued walking through the maze of rooms and corridors, "Are you hungry or anything?"

"What should I expect at sixty meters? Do you have tea?"

Eirene sneered and half turned her head while walking in front of Mark, "Of course I have tea." She continued walking, "From what region? Spiced tea, black tea, green tea, Chinese tea, whatever type you want. I'll show you to the kitchen shortly and you can choose for yourself."

Mark began to follow, "How about Malaysian black tea?"

"I have that, but it was the Dutch and British who introduced it before being Malaysian black tea."

Mark looked in the first room and saw a vast number of oak barrel casks with labels of wine, whiskey, rum, whale oil, kegs of beer, open vats of spices of all colors and scents. "Wine cellar?"

"Not so much wine I'm afraid, but all kinds of useful stores. Next is the library. I've collected an assortment of books over the years including logbooks from various sunken vessels and some captain's caps, even a wooden leg." She pointed into the next room, "The dining room."

Mark looked in and saw a vast mahogany table with matching chairs. The walls were adorned with some of the most precious painters' works. The paintings were in glass cases to protect them against the humidity. Dresser drawers overflowed with silverware of various cultures; ivory handles, horn handles, stacked linen table clothes, and napkins grouped in patterns on shelves. "Do you have enough of everything? You look like a cultured collector or a hoarder."

"Yes, it looks that way, but if you knew the stories behind such items, you would think differently. This is another store room. It includes cases of aged Belgian beer, Scotch Whiskey, Tequila, Mongolian Vodka and even real Absinthe. Next is the kitchen."

6

Most everyone remained along the guardrails, searching for Mark. Robyn remained up the mast. It had been two hours since Mark was last seen and the boat and crew had gone quiet and the guests began murmuring worst case scenarios. Kylie gave details over the satellite phone talking to the Indonesian Coast Guard, her dive company, Mark's dive insurance company, and the authorities in the closest inhabited island towns. With the AIS turned on, the captain and his first mate spoke on separate radios and channels to passing vessels, giving their location, their situation, and informing everyone to be on the lookout for a man overboard. One skiff had been sent off with extra petrol to follow the current with two extra people on board to search for Mark or his body floating adrift in the middle of the sea. Chris prepared his dive kit with Scott, the other tech diver, keeping Chris company and reviewing deep dive procedures. Scott's dive kit was set up with two tanks and ready for any emergency but Raoul was diving again. Sari and Sophie, the other two dive guides, resupplied the smaller first aid kit and took inventory of the bigger kit for reordering purposes. Their dive kits were also set up and ready to assist in either a rescue of an injured victim or a body retrieval. All experienced and able divers were ready and at Kylie's beck and call. The only person not on deck was Raoul.

Raoul sat in his cabin downloading the video from his camera to his computer to enhance the footage. As he watched his screen, he could easily see four legs, relaxed and trailing like an iguana swimming with the tail propelling the creature through the water. He split the screen and went to his fish identification application and started scrolling through eels and snakes just to be sure. He was outside internet range and couldn't google strange animal sightings in the area. He watched the footage frame-by-frame and came to the conclusion that this was a newly discovered species. He began thinking of what this footage would do for his underwater photography career. He realized that he and Chris had to go back down to collect the tanks that they had placed earlier. He began recharging his camera battery and continued looking at the footage over and over.

7

With a cup of black tea in Mark's hand, Eirene took him deeper into the labyrinth. Mark walked past a collection of multicolored Japanese blown glass floats and a collection of old deep sea diving helmets set in a row on a shelf. She turned into the next room and said, "This is a miscellaneous collection room."

Mark looked up at the numerous crystal chandeliers and oil lamps hanging from the ceiling. Mariner and extinct country flags overlapped on the walls like scales. The shelves surrounding a second dining table were filled with porcelain bowls, plates, cups, and saucers. Silverware again filled the drawers. Crystal pitchers and glasses, pewter mugs, and porcelain wash basins filled an open cabinet. "Wow! This stuff should be in a museum."

Eirene agreed, "It is. This whole place is a museum."

"You say you collected these items?" Mark said with a grin.

Mark's perspective faded as Eirene winced at him, "I didn't steal them if that's what you're implying. And it's not stealing if they're already dead." She shrugged and continued, "Some were gifts from the occasional suitor wanting more than just me; as if I wasn't enough for any man." She raised her hands over her head and spun a pirouette before walking back toward the hallway. "Some owners had no further use for them. And some were too valuable to let bury and decay in the deep. I brought some here. Some are safe elsewhere. It's kind of like shopping. If you want something bad enough, you just have to be willing to pay the price and it's not always money. Life can be currency."

In another room, Mark saw compasses and collapsible telescopes. Bones and skulls of both animals and humans locked in glass cabinets. Tiger, leopard and bear pelts were attached to the walls. Ivory tusks, tapestries, more paintings, carvings, masks, and shields were all stacked in rows. Sculptures and full sets of armor stood motionless in the corners. As Eirene and Mark moved into the next room she announced, "And here's part of my treasury." Treasure chests filled with gold and silver coins lined a wall. Chinese beer barrels brimmed with rubies, diamonds, sapphires, semi-precious stones, jewels and jewelry. Mark saw colonial weapons, swords, helmets, stacks of silver and gold bars, coins with Kublai Khan's head on one side, and barrels of pink, black and white pearls. Mark continued to follow Eirene through the maze of rooms and corridors.

Eirene looked back at Mark. "This is going to sound very awkward, but I have a proposition for you. What if I told you I could get you safely back to the surface and back on your boat within twenty-four hours? But you have to do something for me."

"I'd say that's great. What do I have to do?"

"Well." Watching Mark's face, "I'll just be honest with you." Eirene sighed, preparing herself for her confession. "My children are mostly dead due to vessel traffic, climate change, and overabundance of plastic garbage, ghost drift nets, your barbarian wars and so on. I want more children and I want you to share my bed with me, and I don't mean sleep. If you refuse, you will be here until you consent, or I just kill you now and your present reality on the surface fades into Robyn's memory at best." She pointed the tip of her sword at Mark's heart and held it firmly with two hands.

Mark put his hands up and took a step back with a shocked look on his face staring at Eirene.

Eirene stepped forward and pushed the tip of her blade harder into Mark's chest and sternly explained "I'm not asking you to love me. I don't even want to keep you. I want you to go back to your boat and go about your life. Go travel with your girlfriend when the expedition is over. I could probably help influence that outcome as well, if you really want her. Then you forget about your experience down here and never mention it to anyone. Ever."

Mark argued, "Of course I want her, but this proposition of yours goes against my relationship with Robyn."

Eirene replied nonchalantly, "Not anymore it doesn't. You said it yourself, your relationship isn't really consummated and she doesn't have to know what happens in the deep. If you want her, then we do this and you're free to go. I'll guarantee your safe return and she'll be at your side for the rest of her life. Do we have an arrangement?"

"I need to get back on that boat. Once again, you're giving me no options."

She pulled her sword away and put it back in its sheath. "That's true." She tilted her head for Mark to follow her and walked into another room. There was a raised teak bed with a cream linen canopy, white sheets and a rolled up duvet. She took a towel off a rack near an open spring spillway and handed it to Mark. "I'll find you a sarong or something." Eirene headed out of the room.

When Mark looked back Eirene was gone. He stood in his wet board shorts in disbelief.

Eirene re-entered the room shortly and handed a sarong to Mark, "You can leave your shorts here to dry. To be honest with you, I'm not like humans. I haven't had a child in a long time. You are giving me that opportunity and I thank you for it."

8

Kylie climbed the mast and explained to Robyn what was going to happen for the next few days then she climbed down, leaving Robyn to continue searching. Kylie went to ring the bell for everyone to assemble on the top deck for an update briefing. People emerged from all over the boat and came to the upper deck and sat down, waiting anxiously and whispering amongst themselves. Within earshot of Kylie, some continued looking out over the ocean hoping for a glimpse of color.

Kylie began, "Okay, everybody, listen up. As you are aware, we are in an emergency situation with Mark missing. The skiffs are still out searching the surface for any signs of him. Eventually, he will surface and we want to find him and bring him back to the boat, hopefully alive. As the clock ticks, our window for his survival is closing or has already closed. You all would want us to do the same for you, so be patient and understanding. The coast guard is too far away to be of any use and the passage is too narrow for their vessel anyway. Mark's insurance company cannot help us because we are too remote. We have notified passing ferries, fishing boats, any ships traveling in either direction of this passage between the two islands. We are on our own out here and we have to stay with it for a few more days. I'm sorry for the expedition interruption but it has to be done. Some of our divers are still interested in removing the net and we need to retrieve two tanks that Chris and Raoul left below for Mark just in case he got that far. While we are evaluating and discussing our options, the rest of you will go over your gear. You are going to learn how to clean your own gear and change 'O' rings if damaged or corrosion is present. When we are on board, Chris, Sophie, and myself will be assisting you with your gear if there is nothing more pressing. Don't close up any equipment without our inspection and then we'll test it before going back in the water. Chris and Raoul will go down when the current begins to slow, in an hour or so. Snacks are coming up shortly and let's stay attentive on the sea in both directions just in case. The captain, his mate and I will continue calling for assistance and information. Tanks have been lowered at each end of the ship for anyone getting close to deco or running low on air, or for Mark. There isn't a lot more we can do, so let's stay with it until the situation changes. Okay. Thank you for your time."

9

Mark wandered into the library and it began to glow. He walked along the walls of shelves looking at book titles separated into numerous languages. On one shelf there was a thick row of tattered ship logbooks. He looked at the names of the vessels and the dates on the spine. He pulled out an East India Company logbook from the 1700s and flipped it open and began reading some of the entries. There were daily dates, recorded times, latitudes and longitudes, and weather conditions written at the top of each entry. Entries ranged from duties of the day to events and sightings of other vessels. As he turned the pages he read a short clip about the night watchmen apparently seeing a woman in the ocean. Mark read on a few days later, the night watchmen had fallen overboard and went missing. Key crew member disappearances followed. He read on; the remaining crew, the mate and captain, all witnessed a woman in the water surrounded by dolphins. The record tells of the vessel taking on water and the crew that was forced to abandon ship and man the lifeboats. The last entry described overturned lifeboats and screams in the night.

Mark put the logbook back and grabbed another one and sat down in a chair and opened it. He read the beginning, the vessel's port of call, its cargo, number of crew members, destination, estimated date of arrival, and again, latitudes and longitudes as they made entries along their course. Mark only read English so his logbook choices were limited but he suspected the stories would have a similar fatal demise. Mark came to the disturbing conclusion that Eirene had been the cause of many ships and crews lost at sea, never to be seen or heard from again. She had been described as a "taunting mermaid" for hundreds of years. His hair went up on his neck and goosebumps raised on his forearms. Panic struck Mark and all he could think about was escaping and getting back to Robyn and the ship. He was convinced Eirene planned to kill him now that she had what she wanted and he was a loose end she could tie off easy enough.

Mark went down to the small beach and cave and saw two more dive tanks set against the cave wall. He picked them up and knew they were full by their weight. He put them down and checked his Surface Marker Buoy line. He retrieved the line and saw it had been cut. Not knowing if the Eolian would still be there, it was a gamble to try to ascend via the sea considering he still wasn't done with his decompression and would need more time to release nitrogen through his lungs as he ascended. He couldn't calculate it but his computer would be close. His mind spun off in different fear-stricken directions. He looked at his dive computer again. He still had a few hours left before he could attempt an escape thinking Eirene wouldn't keep her end of the bargain. He decided to explore the entire recesses of the labyrinth. Mark felt trapped. He thought she wouldn't care what he explored as long as he did his part. He could think of no other way to stall her as he moved about. He needed time.

10

As Caroline and Scott led two groups down at slack tide to remove the net and pile it on a skiff, Chris, Raoul, Sari and Sophie, dived down to retrieve the two tanks. There was no current as the four dropped off the wall into the blue. They were scanning the wall and Chris saw where he had put the extra tank, he even saw the heel print of the tank in the sediment. He looked over at Raoul who was shaking his head while pointing where he had put the other tank. Raoul's camera was filming as they went. Sophie and Sari looked down the wall with their torches searching for bubbles or signs of life. A dark shadow passed in the deep. Sophie pinged her tank as she followed the shadow with her light. It disappeared in the distance. Chris knew they were running out of time and called the dive back to the surface. The sea dragon came straight up the wall and bit Raoul on the arm. It let go and went straight back into the deep. Raoul put air in his BCD and began to go up before he passed out. Chris saw Raoul's limp arms and legs with his head hanging down and went over and found him unresponsive. He waived Sari over to help control Raoul's ascent and they all went up together. Sari held Raoul's regulator in his mouth while Sophie continued searching for the creature and for Mark. Raoul was breathing shallowly on his own so they continued in a controlled ascent kicking up slower than their bubbles. Sophie saw the shadow moving back and forth but not coming closer. As they came to the edge of the wall, Sophie noticed a woman's head peering over a rock wall twenty meters below them. The woman had no tank but was calmly watching them as they stopped for a safety stop. Sophie pinged her tank and pointed. Chris and Sari looked back to where she was pointing and watched the woman disappear behind the rocks and the shadow followed her out of sight.

The skiff was standing by when the divers surfaced. Chris explained to the driver, "Call the Eolian and setup the 100% oxygen tank and the larger first aid kit to Raoul's room for an injury."

Raoul was still limp but he had a pulse and was breathing. They boarded the skiff and sped off toward the Eolian.

Sophie shook her head in disbelief and asked, "What did we just see?"

Chris was looking at Raoul's bite mark oozing blood and replied, "I don't know. Maybe a giant eel."

Sari looked at Chris and said, "I don't think it's an eel. It had legs."

Chris looked up at the two women and said calmly, "I don't know what we saw but let's take a minute and fix Raoul before we start talking out of our heads to the others. Let's stabilize Raoul then get together and figure it out. Okay?"

Sophie exclaimed, "And the woman! I saw a woman with no tank down there. How can that be?"

Chris again tried to get them to focus, "Mark and Raoul are our priority. Stay with me on this. We all saw her and we'll talk together later. Okay? This is serious for us and the dive company. Right now, it's a giant eel that bit Raoul. Sophie, you play with cameras and computers the most. Maybe you and Sari can have a look at Raoul's camera and make heads or tails of what's going on down there before we tell the others. Agreed?"

They both nodded and started pulling off their gear as they approached the Eolian. The two deckhands were standing by to assist in Raoul's transfer to his room.

11

Mark walked up through the labyrinth quietly carrying his dive gear and came to Eirene's bed chamber and looked in. He put his gear down outside her entry and walked in. Eirene wasn't in bed. Mark called out. There was no response. He dropped the sarong, put on his board shorts and walked back out ... then he picked up his gear and walked up a path he had not yet explored. It wound around like a large coil constantly turning to the right until the path came to a bleak room with a teak coffee table and four chairs. The room was hot and humid with condensation dripping down the walls. He put his dive gear in a chair and walked the perimeter of the room expecting to find a hidden passage onward. He looked at his dive computer and noticed he had almost completed his decompression. Seeing no way out, Mark turned, grabbed his dive gear and headed back down toward the cave entrance to get the two tanks and escape.

As he rounded the bend, Eirene threw a glass of slime on Mark's face and in his eyes and said, "Leaving without saying good-bye? Thank you for your company. Your time is almost complete and you are no longer welcome. Do not mention this place, nor of me, and never come down here again or I will kill you and everybody on your ship. Understand?"

"I understand." Mark went numb, dropped to his knees and limply fell on his face.

12

Chris knocked on Sari and Sophie's cabin door.

Sari opened the door and let Chris in and asked, "How's Raoul?"

Chris replied, "He's stitched up, but can't take fluids because he's in a deep sleep or something. His vitals are stable and now we are in a situation between getting Raoul to a hospital or continuing to search for Mark's body. He's surely dead. Kylie called a meeting in about fifteen minutes for all instructors, including guest instructors. All three of us are to attend. How'd you go with the footage?"

Sophie started the video over and said, "Sari and I are sure it's not an eel. It's nothing I've ever seen before. It's bigger, it doesn't swim like an eel, and you'll see the shape of its head as it bites Raoul's arm. There's also a short clip of the woman. I've been trying to freeze it on her but it's only a frame or two. It's definitely a woman with no dive gear. Sophie played the video from their descent. The video showed no tanks on the wall then shook back and forth focusing in Chris's direction. In the background, a figure's head appeared. Sophie froze the video and moved frame to frame until she was in focus.

Chris uttered slowly, "Holy shit. That is definitely a person's head." He looked at Sari.

Sari nodded in agreement, "That's what we said too, but where's her dive gear or air tank? Maybe she's the one who took the boat tanks."

Chris offered an alternative, "Or maybe Mark got them and went with the current. There's no way of knowing yet."

Sophie started the video again and they watched as they ascended to the surface. With Raoul's head down, the shadow of the sea creature could be seen vaguely in the distant blue below them.

"Come on. It is nearly sunset. We'll look at this again later. Right now we need to go to the meeting and figure out how to proceed. Kylie should be finished talking on the horn to a couple medical centers for additional information and to Raoul's insurance company for a second patient. Raoul and Mark come first. Let's be sure of these video shots before showing them to the others. We want to stay focused and not add more stress and tension than necessary." Chris walked out the door with Sari following him.

Sophie powered down her computer leaving the data card in the computer and followed the others to the top deck.

Robyn had come down from the mast and sat with her feet dangling over the edge of the ship. Her chin rested on the guardrail crossbeam while watching the sunset with wet eyes. Other guests walked past her in silence on their way to listen to Kylie.

Kylie had commandeered the center table and removed all but eight chairs. She had put down sheets of paper and pens for everyone. Chris, Sari, Sophie, Caroline—guest instructor from England, Scott Bentley—guest Dive Master from San Diego, the captain, and his first mate came to the table. Kylie watched as the guests came up and sat around the perimeter cushions on the benches. Once everybody was settled, Kylie announced, "Hey everybody. I don't mind that you are here. You are more than welcome to listen in but I don't want any interruptions or talking up here besides us at the table. I'm sorry but it's too distracting. At the end of our meeting I will allow you to ask questions or offer alternative suggestions, but not until the end please. That being said, let's begin with the situation at hand. Raoul is in stable condition but with an infection rapidly spreading up his arm and moving toward his chest and heart. We are not certified or authorized to give antibiotics or fluids intravenously, so we need him to wake up before we can administer anything at this point. The captain has charted a course for the closest medical center with an airport in case of any unforeseen complication or additional emergencies. That harbor is Alor and is approximately three days away without stops or delays by bad weather. I think we can save Raoul if we go directly. The sad and tragic side of that decision is postponing or altogether abandoning the search for Mark. Mark was last seen more than twenty-four hours ago. The two skiffs have scoured the coastlines on both islands and done grid searches on both sides of the tides in this channel. With all our eyes glued to the surface water, we have seen no signs of Mark. Best case scenario for Mark is that he made it to shore or got picked up by a boat, but we have had no communications as such. Worst case scenario, Mark ran out of air, suffocated and drowned. With his weight belt and water in his lungs, he'd be on the bottom for a few days and then he'll biologically gas up to the surface and hopefully be found."

The guests sat quietly tearing up and shyly looking for Robyn. Robyn's tears fell into a red sunset.

Kylie watched Robyn get up and go below toward her cabin not wanting to hear the logical choice. The sun dropped over the horizon.

Kylie continued, "I want to hear from everybody around this table on how you would proceed and our options. Remember your training and unfortunately, triage. Do we potentially lose two guests or save one?"

Robyn went down the stairs to her cabin. There was water on the hallway floor and a set of footprints leading into her room. She cleared her eyes as she walked to her door and listened. There was someone inside and it wasn't Caroline. She opened the door and found a woman placing Mark on Caroline's bed.

Eirene turned and quickly pulled Robyn inside and closed the door. "Are you Robyn?"

Robyn saw Mark's limp body. A whole new wave of emotions gripped her heart. "Is he alive?"

"Yes. Are you Robyn?"

Confused, squinting her eyes and shaking her head, "Ye-yes."

"Good. Listen carefully, Robyn."

Robyn tried to go to Mark.

Eirene blocked her, pushing Robyn firmly against the door and holding her there with a forearm across the chest and her other hand firmly pointing her sword at Robyn's throat. "Look at me and listen to me. Mark has the same sickness as the other man. He should wake up some time late tonight. You take care of him. Stay with him. Forever. You say nothing of me to the others. If you do, I'll kill everybody on board. Do you promise me?"

Not understanding what was happening, Robyn tried to nod and wipe a new stream of tears from her cheeks.

"Good. I'm going to hold you to your promise by taking away your fertility. Next time we meet, I'll give it back. Deal?" Eirene ripped Robyn's shirt up and palmed her abdomen. When she finished Eirene moved her sword point away from Robyn's throat.

"You're going to do what!? I don't understand."

"You will in time. I need you to do something for me. When you get home to San Francisco, take Mark to Chinatown. He will meet someone there that can explain a lot to both of you."

"What?"

"Just do it," Eirene said sternly and continued, "Things will be more clear after you do this. Are we all good here?"

Robyn nodded.

Eirene put her sword away. "I don't have much time. Where are the camera videos from down below?"

"I don't know anything about any videos," replied Robyn.

"Where are the rooms for the women and men that came down?"

Robyn pointed through the wall and explained, "The women guides sleep next door and Chris and Kylie are at the end on the right. Raoul is in his room, one deck up at the back of the ship. He's sleeping and his arm is infected."

"Thanks. Everything will be fine if you keep your mouth shut. See you later." Eirene released Robyn and opened the door pushing Robyn directly to Mark's bedside.

Robyn looked at Mark and noticed he had changed, he looked younger. She watched him breathing while listening to the noises next door. The next door shut and foot pads sounded down the hallway, then nothing. Robyn felt Mark's check with the back of her hand, then checked his pulse on his neck. She took off his wet rash guard and board shorts and grabbed a blanket and put it over him. She looked out the door in both directions only to see wet footprints heading back up the stairs. She closed her door and went back to Mark's side. He was definitely younger. She pulled the blanket back and looked at his stomach. It was more defined with a six-pack of trim muscles. She put her hand over her mouth in disbelief.

The engine started up and the anchor chain chimed link after link as the crew weighed anchor. Robyn composed herself, wiping away streaks of tears, she walked out of the room and up the stairs to the others on the top deck. Kylie was the first to greet her and apologized, "I'm so sorry, Robyn. We made the choice to take Raoul to Alor."

Robyn cut her off, "It's okay. I don't know how it happened but Mark is on board. He's in Caroline's bed right now. I think he has the same thing Raoul does. I tried to wake him up but I couldn't." Tears welled up in Robyn's eyes again.

Kylie spun around searching faces, "Chris, Sophie, grab the small first aid kit and meet me in Robyn's cabin, ASAP!" Kylie ran off down the stairs with Chris and Sophie running to the wheelhouse.

All eyes were on Robyn as she looked at the inquisitive faces sitting around on the top deck. She pointed down the stairs trembling and announced, "Mark is in my room, in Caroline's bed, passed out, like Raoul. Caroline, can you sleep somewhere else tonight, please. I want to take care of Mark."

"Sure. I'll take Mark's bed." Caroline looked at Tom and asked, "If that's all right with you, Tom?"

Tom replied, "Yep. We can talk proper English for a change. Share a few laughs and stories from our homeland."

Caroline teased through a smile, "Or maybe start one or two of our own."

Tom chuckled and said, "Ah yeah, here we go."

Everybody on the deck cheered and laughed, not only at Tom and Caroline's candor but relieved at Mark's return.

Sari walked up to Robyn and handed her a beer. "You look like you could use one of these."

Robyn reached out, "Thanks. Where are we headed? Alor?"

"Yep, off to Alor to get Raoul to a clinic. His infection in his arm is getting worse. How about Mark? Was he bitten?"

"No. Just passed out."

"You sure?"

"Pretty sure." Robyn smiled and winked at Sari.

"Oh. It's like that, is it?" Sari smiled back and they tapped bottles.

Downstairs in Robyn's room, Kylie, Chris, and Sophie took Mark's vitals and concluded, as Robyn had mentioned, he was in a deep sleep similar to Raoul but with no infection visible.

Sophie exclaimed, "Look at his face. It's changed. He looks younger."

Kylie looked closer at his face, "Oh my god! You're right. He's also really pale."

Chris said, "Well, at least he wasn't bitten by that thing."

Kylie looked puzzled and asked, "Why do you say that thing? You already said it was an eel."

Sophie admitted, "Kylie, we don't actually know what it was. At first, we thought it was an eel. But then, when it got closer, we knew it wasn't." Sophie saw Chris nodding in agreement.

Kylie folded her arms and asked, "Why do you say that?"

Chris explained, "It had four legs and was much bigger than any eel I've ever seen."

Kylie looked perplexed, "What are you saying? What do you think it was?"

Chris replied, "We don't know. Sari, Sophie, Raoul and I all saw it. And when Raoul wakes up, he's going to tell you exactly the same thing. It'll be word for word what I'm telling you now. Sari researched through the species identification books and the ID apps and she couldn't find anything like it. So did Raoul after our first dive."

Sophie looked at Chris and suggested, "Maybe it's time to show Kylie Raoul's videos?"

"You have proof? I want to see it. Why didn't you mention it before?"

Chris answered as he opened the door and entered the corridor followed by Sophie and Kylie, "We wanted confirmation and not to start on imagination alone."

Sophie opened her door and walked in, turned on her computer and sat down.

Chris explained, "We took Raoul's data chip out of his camera to see what he and I had seen swimming around when we dropped the tanks and he videoed more when we went to retrieve them. The first video is on Raoul's computer. The second video shows the creature and then, even more disturbing, a woman without dive gear watching us from behind some rock and coral. At that point, Raoul was bitten."

Impatiently, Kylie replied, "Whatever. Okay, so where is the video?"

Sophie looked at her computer and the chip was gone. "I swear, I turned the computer off to go to your meeting and left the chip in the slot. Someone has removed it. Let me go ask Sari. Be right back. I'll bring her down and you can see it and hear it from her." Sophie got up and walked out of the room.

"Okay Chris, explain as best you can exactly what you saw. Everything. No screwing around."

Chris sat on a bed and explained, "When Raoul and I went down with the two tanks and placed them on a ledge, a creature was swimming back and forth below us. Raoul filmed it. I told him to stay with the program and concentrate on rescuing Mark. We would have time to figure out what we saw later. He agreed. Later he looked at the footage and thought it might be an undiscovered species. When the four of us went back down for one last search for Mark and retrieve the tanks, the tanks were gone. Raoul was filming and all four of us saw the creature swimming. Then, it came up and attacked Raoul and disappeared back into the deep. Raoul passed out almost immediately and, as we were coming up, Sophie pinged her tank and pointed to a woman hiding behind the rocks below us. We all saw her, plain as day. It was a woman, for sure, with no gear and no bubbles. I figure she took the tanks, or at best, Mark got them. But when I saw her, I knew we had swum into something beyond our knowledge and that's all we have."

Sophie and Sari came into the room. Sophie blurted, "She doesn't have it either."

Sari explained in her defense, "I walked out after Chris. We've all been upstairs ever since."

Kylie responded, "Obviously, somebody has been in here. Who's been down here?"

Chris answered, "Only Robyn. Everybody else was up at the briefing. And Mark is in no condition to do anything. Where's Robyn? Maybe, Sophie, you could ask her nicely and see where that leads us. Somebody has it on board this ship. It's the only proof we have of what we saw."

13

It was the middle of the night. The engine hummed as the ship followed the swell. Robyn lay in her bed watching Mark as moonlight through a porthole shined and moved like a pendulum across his blanket. She wondered about the woman and what she had said. Now she looked at Mark as her lifelong partner and calmed with that knowledge, as if under a spell.

Mark stirred and raised a hand to his eyes.

Robyn sat up and whispered, "Mark?"

Startled, Mark turned and saw Robyn through the moonlight. He took a deep breath and paused trying to remember how he got there. "Hey. What the hell happened?"

Robyn got up and quietly went to Mark and gave him a hug, "We thought you were dead. Raoul got bit by an eel or something and he's in bad shape. We searched for you for a long time and Kylie and the guides made the decision to get Raoul to a clinic in Alor. We're heading there now. They were abandoning the search for you to save Raoul. I walked in the room when that woman dropped you off."

Shocked, Mark looked at Robyn and asked, "You met her?"

"Met her? She shoved me against the door and put a sword to my throat." In the moonlight, Robyn saw Mark's face. "Mark, your eyes."

Ignoring Robyn, Mark asked in a whisper, "What did she say to you?"

"She asked me my name, threatened me, told me she'd kill me and the others if I spoke of her. She told me some stuff about us and to keep a promise until we meet again."

"Did you say anything to the others?"

"No, of course not. There was no time and now I can't."

"Don't ever mention her to anyone. She doesn't exist. She was never here. We have to cover her up and get off the ship and the sea as fast as possible."

Robyn placed her fingers gently on Mark's lips and calmly said, "Take it easy. As I said, we're on our way to Alor. Kylie says it's the first town with a clinic and an airport."

Mark took another deep breath and admitted, "We really don't have a choice, do we?"

Robyn hugged Mark as he lay there. "No. Not unless you want to swim for it. But there's more to tell you and show you tomorrow. Rest for now." Robyn paused and added, "I think she took Raoul's data chip from his camera. People have been looking for it tonight." Robyn lay down next to Mark and held him."

Mark looked at the Moon as it passed the porthole and responded, "Her name is Eirene."

14

In the morning, there was a knock on the cabin. Robyn got up and opened the door, "Hey, Kylie." Robyn backed up and sat on her bed.

Kylie walked in looking at Mark, "Morning, Robyn. Everything okay last night?"

Robyn shrugged, "Yeah, pretty good. He's been dropping in and out of sleep since about midnight."

Kylie asked, "Did he say or ask for anything?"

Robyn answered, "He's asked me to get him water a couple times and I walked him to the bathroom once."

Kylie picked up Mark's water bottle and asked, "Do you mind getting him some more water?" She handed the bottle to Robyn.

Mark interrupted, "I'd really love a cup of tea, if you would, please."

Robyn got up. "No problem. Be back in a few." Robyn walked out of the room and glanced at Mark.

Before the door closed Kylie blurted, "Have a cup of coffee before you come back down. I want to talk to him alone for a bit."

Robyn cracked the door. "Can I drop off his tea first?"

Mark spoke loudly to Robyn while looking at Kylie, "Yes, please."

Robyn closed the door.

Kylie looked at Mark and asked, "How you feeling?" She held Mark's wrist and took his pulse looking at her watch.

Mark pulled up the covers. "I'm gaining my strength. I'm still exhausted from the swim."

Kylie then asked, "How about your memory? Do you remember what happened?"

"Vaguely. I'm still putting pieces together."

Kylie explained, "We searched for you for almost twenty-four hours. We did surface grids in both directions of the tide. Chris and Raoul went down and searched off the wall and dropped tanks for you, when they went back with Sophie and Sari to do one last search and retrieve the tanks, the tanks were gone and Raoul was bitten by something. We saw no signs of you on the surface and only an eel or something in the deep. Now we have a lot of questions starting with how you managed to get back on board this boat without being seen?"

Mark started, "Well."

Chris walked in with Mark's tea and water bottle, and handed them to him, "I want to hear this too. You good, Mark?"

"Hey Chris. Yeah, I'm fine. I was just explaining what I can remember. There are still a lot of gaps but, I remember dropping in the water with you, Pierre, and Caroline. We found the large net, you assigned us positions and we went to them. The current was picking up. I was getting ready to unsnag the net from the cliff when I noticed a lot of straightened hooks. Then the current surged, I lost my grip and tumbled into the deep. I loaded my BCD but it didn't help, the current was too strong. I saw you and Pierre in an upcurrent. Caroline was in the shallows hanging on the net leader line to the tree. I grabbed at the cliff wall at some point and tried to climb and kick back up. I broke loose and went down to something like one hundred meters and started to pass out. Last visual was at about one hundred and ten meters and the current seemed to lessen. I can't really remember what happened next. Since my BCD was loaded, I think it saved me and brought me up slowly against the current. I woke up at twenty meters and I was out of air. I sucked air out of my BCD manual hose as I came up. When I got to the surface, I reloaded my BCD and passed out, probably due to decompression sickness. I should be dead. The Moon gave me a bit of light and I drifted with the current and woke up in the rocks. My only guess is there is a whirlpool effect on the back side of the island. I really don't know. I couldn't see the ship or anything. I remember sleeping on the rocks during part of the day and woke up briefly yesterday afternoon. The rocks were too jagged to walk on so I stayed in the shallows and swam around the edge of the island. I rested until the tide and current went toward the boat then swam along the cliffs again. Just before the current was going to change, I swam straight for the boat. I climbed in a skiff, pulled the skiff to the stern and climbed on board. Next thing I knew, I was here and Robyn was sleeping there." Mark sighed and continued, "Thanks for the tea, Chris. Kylie said something about Raoul being bitten by something. Is he okay?"

Chris nodded and replied, "Yeah, he's going to be fine. He's got an infected arm, but he'll survive. Did you see anything down there? Sharks, eels, two air tanks, anything?"

Mark shook his head and explained, "I wasn't really looking around. I think I heard dolphins or something when I was clinging to the cliff, but really, I was more concerned with self-preservation at that point, not marine life."

Kylie looked at her feet for a second wondering how far she could go and asked, "I'm just curious here but, how did your gear get back in its bin?"

Mark shrugged and answered, "I don't remember. Maybe Robyn picked it up off the back deck and put it away. I was so out of it and exhausted, I just came straight in here and laid down. I didn't even make it to my own cabin."

Kylie nodded and responded suspiciously, "Okay, maybe so. I'll be sure to ask Robyn about the gear."

Caroline knocked on the door and opened it, simultaneously announcing, "Excuse me. Just thought you should know, Raoul is awake. Sophie is with him now getting some fluids and antibiotics in him. Welcome back, Mark."

"Hey, Caroline. Thanks. And thanks for the use of your bed."

Caroline smiled and said, "Oh, no problem. It's been quite a night for both of us."

Kylie laughed and said, "Okay, that's enough information. Thanks Caroline. We'll be along in a few minutes. Can you tell Robyn to come back down when she's free?"

"Sure. I'll let her know." Caroline shut the door with a grin and went back upstairs.

Chris turned to leave, "Kylie, I'm going to go check something. I'll meet you at Raoul's room."

Kylie nodded, "Okay."

"Mark, you rest up and I'll come check on you later." Chris went out the door.

"Alright. Thanks."

Kylie concluded, "I should go too and check on Raoul and listen to what he has to say while he's awake. Robyn will be back soon and I'll talk to you later."

"Yeah, alright. There isn't much more to tell."

"We'll see." Kylie went out the door and headed upstairs and onto the deck where Chris was having a cigarette.

Chris saw Kylie and went to her. "You're not going to believe this but all the tanks are accounted for, Mark's tank and the two tanks Raoul and I took down."

Kylie shook her head. "That's not possible. We're missing something,"

Chris replied, "Yeah, or someone."

15

ONE WEEK LATER

Robyn and Mark walked from the Transamerica Pyramid, up Merchant Street into San Francisco's Chinatown. Red lanterns crisscrossed high above the streets. Fragrant incense smoldered in doorways and at small shrines. Shops and restaurants bustled with locals and tourists. Roasted ducks hung on display in restaurant and shop windows. After walking to the center of Chinatown on the hill, Mark stopped abruptly in front of a Chinese restaurant and looked in the entrance. It was unusually dim inside considering the fog had burned off and the sun shined brightly overhead.

Robyn looked at Mark while explaining, "Eirene told me to bring you here to meet someone and that they will help make sense of what's happening to you, the physical changes and stuff. Not that I mind, mind you. You're fit and look like a boy toy for a rich cougar. I'm still working on the rich part but I've got the cougar bit down." Robyn smiled and reached for Mark's hand. "Are you getting a feeling?"

"Yeah, I am." Mark looked at Robyn and pointed inside the restaurant, "There's someone I'm supposed to meet in there. It's weird. I just get a sensation and really curious. I can feel someone is in there and vice-versa. They know I'm here."

"You're buying Chinese for lunch then. Lead the way, boy toy."

Mark smiled at Robyn and said, "I just don't know what to expect."

Robyn suggested, "Let's start with a couple menus and take it from there. It's the next step in the adventure. Come on." They started walking toward the entrance when Robyn added, "I hope you have money because I'm not doing any dishes in there."

Mark smiled and walked into the dimly lit restaurant and answered over his shoulder, "Yeah, and you're the one with the cushy employment contract. I think you need to pay me more, Miss Engineer."

Robyn replied, looking at Mark's back, "I'll take it under consideration. But you have to prove your worth, horizontally speaking, of course."

"You name where and when."

"Right here." Robyn picked a central four top table and sat down facing the front door. Mark sat opposite looking toward the kitchen and restroom doors. The restaurant was narrow with only ten tables and high rectangular windows facing an adjacent graffiti-laden concrete wall. A few tables of Chinese businessmen were gorging themselves on various small dish delicacies along with bowls of different sauces and vegetables. There was a pot of steamed rice in the middle of each feeding frenzy.

Mark listened to all the clattering of plates and utensils mixed with Chinese words pinballing around in his ears and said to Robyn, "You were really fortunate getting a job so fast. Sometimes, it takes months, years even to get what you want."

Robyn opened her menu and agreed, "Yeah. Well, I've been in contact with them since you got back on board and the boat headed for Alor. I called them, then emailed my resume from Labuan Bajo, and started video chat interviews since then. If I wasn't hired by them, I would have taken a lesser paying job, like I said, just to get my foot in the door and wait for an opening. Have you thought anymore about managing my uncle's bookstore? He really could use a year off and we can use the time to figure out our future plans."

Mark nodded and answered, "For now, it sounds great. But, I don't think I could do it long term. I'll commit to one year to start with and see how it goes."

"Good. We can contact him tomorrow with the good news and it gives you a starting point."

A man approached with a pitcher of water and two glasses. As he poured the water he greeted them, "Welcome. I just thought I'd tell you our special in case you missed it out front or don't read Cantonese. Each person orders five dishes off the list on the wall." He pointed at a banner listing numerous dishes in Cantonese and English. "It comes with rice, vegetables and sauces so you can play around and see what works for you. It's only ten bucks per person. How does that sound?"

Mark nodded and Robyn said with raised brows and a smile, "We'll have one each and can we get a pot of tea for two?"

"Sure. Great. I'll be back shortly with your tea and give you a chance to decide where you want to start. You don't have to pick them all at once. Pick a few and you can find out what you like and go from there." He walked into the kitchen.

Robyn looked at Mark and asked, "So?"

Mark looked at Robyn and finished the thought, "So, it's not him if that's what you mean. Whoever it is, they're back there." Mark nodded toward the kitchen.

"And it's not any of these people in the restaurant." Robyn shrugged and continued flatly, "Process of elimination. That's the first one we've met who comes and goes from that direction. Now just sit back ... what are you going to have?"

A few minutes later, the waiter came over with the tea and placed it on the table and asked, "Do you have any questions or decisions?"

Robyn ordered, "I'll have number three, five, and seven to start off. I'll save the other two for the next round."

Mark waited until the man stopped writing and ordered, "I'll start with number ten, eleven, and fourteen."

"Great. Anything else?" The waiter looked at Robyn and then Mark.

Mark spoke up, "Sorry, I've got an odd question."

The waiter looked at Mark.

Mark pointed toward the kitchen, "Who's back in there? I don't so much mean the kitchen staff but others?"

"Oh, well, this is a family-run business. One of the oldest in Chinatown. My father has his office back there and my grandfather lives here full time. My grandfather started this business ages ago and the restaurant is still family run."

Robyn responded, "Oh, that's cool, and good for the family to have such support."

Mark added, "Thanks. I was just curious."

"No problem." The waiter walked off through the kitchen double doors.

Robyn stared at Mark, wondering what he was thinking, hoping he was putting the pieces together. Robyn whispered, "I wonder how old she is."

"What do you mean? She's old judging from the logbooks often sighting her in the ocean over the last couple hundred years." Mark stopped talking and looked up at a grinning elderly Chinese man in black dress shoes, tan slacks, a brown cashmere V-neck sweater, and white collared shirt. Mark exclaimed quietly, "It's you."

The elderly man came forward with an outstretched hand, "Nice to meet you, Mark. May I sit down?"

Mark looked shocked as he reached out his hand. "Of course. You know my name?"

"Eirene didn't know when, but she told me you were coming."

Robyn interrupted, "Hello, my name is Robyn." Robyn put out her hand.

"Hello. My name is Hong." Hong accepted Robyn's handshake. "You met her too, Robyn. I can tell. I can feel it from both of you. Yours is going to continue to grow, Robyn."

"I've noticed that to." Mark looked at Robyn. "I'm beginning to feel you when you are near, whether you are coming or going, stuff like that."

Robyn smiled. "Oh really. In that case, I should probably call up my other boyfriends and let them know I'm wearing a tracker."

Hong explained, "Eirene knows where we all are. Her senses are much more acute than ours. We develop and evolve through time. Her senses are fully developed. And you're not even close about her age. I said the same thing you just did, thinking her only a couple hundred years old. Except, I had that thought three hundred years ago." Hong tilted his head side to side and confessed, "A little over, but yes, in general terms."

Robyn asked, "Wait, so, somehow she gave you immortality or something? Mark has been changing ever so slightly since being on the ship in Indonesia."

Hong shook his head and explained, "Not immortality. Longevity. She gave me long life and she gave it to Mark, but yours won't develop until you meet her again. She is happy with the result, you two together and keeping it quiet. You will make a fine addition to the surface allies."

Mark asked, "Allies?"

The waiter came over with a tray of different dishes and all the trimmings and placed them around the table, "Here you go for your first taste testers. Enjoy." The waiter stood with a comically exaggerated look on his face and added, "Grandpa, don't annoy my customers or I'm going to throw you out again."

Hong chuckled and waved off his grandson.

Mark looked at the waiter with a knowing smile. "That won't be necessary." Mark looked at Hong and invited him, "You are welcome to join us. We have questions and we can talk while we eat."

Hong bowed his head and spoke to his grandson in Cantonese before he walked off into the kitchen. Hong looked at Robyn and Mark and began, "If the legends are true and I'm not saying they are or aren't, you still need to take everything you hear with a grain of salt. Only when you witness something yourself or have proof can you believe. When she says she's gone by many names, this is true. Eirene says her mother was a nymph named Melantheia. Melantheia was the daughter of a river god named Alpheus. Melantheia and Poseidon had a baby, Eirene, so says the legends. She's been down there ever since, living a life of bitterness and void of compassion. She has been betrayed by man farther back than any written history. Eirene is supposed to stand for 'Peace' but she is quite the opposite. I have done quite a bit of research and still cannot find the source of her powers."

Mark squinted his eyes in disbelief, "Poseidon? *The* Poseidon. The Greek God of the Sea?"

Hong nodded. "Yes, if you believe in the legends."

Mark scoffed. "That's ridiculous. I can't accept that."

Hong nodded solemnly, "Mark, you believe what you did and witnessed to be true. I have been here well past the normal life span of man, and your body is changing. Is this not true? All this is happening because you and I crossed her path. I do not know the whole truth, but I know what I've seen and done to be true. Maybe you will help us find the whole truth."

Robyn loaded her plate and asked, "How did you meet her? It couldn't have been diving."

Hong smiled and shook his head, "No, not diving. We were following the trade routes and were shipwrecked during a storm. We had been trading, buying and selling everything from spice, pearls, and metals all the way from Sumatra around to China. We were sailing at the tail end of the Ming treasure voyages and had been at sea for two years scratching out a living but never enough to get off the ship without breaking our contracts. Our captain was a well-respected and seasoned officer who, as a young boy, sailed under Admiral Zheng He in the 15th century. This wasn't one of the giant vessels the Chinese constructed carrying fifty sailors and military personnel. Our boat only carried fifteen sailors including some military. We sailed north from Timor to Larantuka, eastern Flores, with a load of sandalwood and a great deal of precious metal ore. After delivery and payment, the captain gave half the crew time off until the following midday. When we returned, my two friends had spent their shore allowance and I only had half mine. The ship had been reloaded to the rails without us. We boarded and all met with the captain. He told us what we were carrying and where we were headed. Supplies had been procured and we set sail with a fully loaded ship on the tide and toward our destination. What started out as a blessing sealed our fate. We made good speed, but a typhoon hit and the waves doubled in size. We were exposed in a strong wind and a breaking rouge wave capsized our ship. We immediately lost a portion of our cargo unbalancing the ship. Another wave hit the hull and the masts and sails tipped into the sea. All the cargo broke loose and fell to the bottom of the ocean. We lost many men as we drifted back out into open water clinging to the remainder of the hull. By morning we had lost almost the entire crew. Good men. The storm continued. There were only four of us left, the captain, the doctor, a crew member, and myself. We tried dropping the sails and righting what was left of the ship, but we had no leverage. It was hard to hang on between the water and waves crashing into the hull repeatedly. Eventually, the boat broke into pieces on jagged rock at the base of a cliff. We had made it to land and got out of the water for the first time in days. The other deckhand was bleeding badly out of his foot and leg. The doctor did his best but my friend bled out and died. We searched for a way out from under the cliff for a time but we were trapped and had to get back in the water and swim for a beach or jungle exit. We swam to the same sandy atoll you were diving near and looked around. It was raining and Eirene came out of the water and stabbed the captain and the doctor, and knocked me out. I woke up in her cave." Hong looked into Mark's eyes and added, "After that, I think our stories are similar."

Robyn added, "That's the part I want to hear. I'm the only one here who has met her but never been in her house."

Mark said frankly, "It's not a house. It's a labyrinth of tunnels gouged out by a millennium of water rushing through it, an underground volcano and uplifted plate tectonics. She didn't need you in her labyrinth because you're a woman and you're not of any interest to her. She blackmailed us into sleeping with her for procreation and promised we'd be able to resume our lives on the surface, keeping a lifelong secret or perishing."

Hong nodded.

Robyn looked at Hong and then Mark for a moment, "You slept with her?"

Mark and Hong both nodded.

"Seriously?" Exaggerating with her eyes wide open Robyn asked, "Is this where the word nymphomaniac comes in to play?"

Hong spoke up. "There's more to it. Yes, it was against our will. She gave us an ultimatum, either do her bidding or remain until submission. She didn't want us; she wanted our seed."

Robyn asked, "I'm having a hard time imagining a man say no in the first place." Robyn was fuming with anger while staring at Mark with daggers in her eyes. A moment passed before she continued, "Okay. So, how many children do you have with her, Hong?"

"From the one day I spent with Eirene, I've personally met six of our children. In time, Mark, you will meet your own."

Robyn continued, "Boy, are you two in trouble, knocking up Poseidon's daughter. I can't wait to see what he does to you." Robyn glanced at Mark and folded her arms. "Seriously?"

Mark confessed, "I'm sorry Robyn. It's true. I'm going to change the subject here, Hong. What did you mean by 'allies'?"

Hong smiled and shook his head, "You and I are not the only two that have been with Eirene. There are more of us and we have slowly been finding each other much like you and I can feel each other's presence. Many have died along the way and also lost all their children to the oceans around the world. Those on land stand a much better chance of living a more than full life than those in the sea considering we are killing the seas and oceans. Robyn, you too, one day will feel my presence and Mark's, and the others when the time comes. You'll lose years and your body will battle all diseases and be given physical adaptations like Mark's. Age becomes a memory, time stands still and living can either be a gift or a curse. It depends on how you handle it." Hong admired Robyn's perspective and continued, "You should know, Robyn, you are the first female that I have ever met that has not died by Eirene's sword."

Robyn nodded and replied, "Good to know. So I'm going to get a six-pack stomach like Mark's and the rest of the package too."

Hong bowed his head and concluded their meeting, "You will get it, Robyn, if you remain true to your promise to Eirene. I thank you both for hearing my story. I believe you two have some talking to do and I have some other matters I need to attend to. It was great to meet you both and now you know where to find me if you have more questions, information or trouble. Oh, and your lunch was on the house. Until next time. Xiè xie." Hong waved as he walked off.

"Xiè xie," Robyn put her hands together touching her forehead and bowing slightly as Hong closed a side door. "Wow. Nice choice of restaurant. Let's give up five bucks for the tip and get out of here. We can talk about this outside. Break out the cash, boy toy, and let's go. Then again, a boy toy that has shagged a nymphomaniac cougar princess looks pretty good on your resume. I'll take it into consideration after your physical review. There's got to be bragging rights in there somewhere." Robyn got up and walked toward the door.

Mark got up to reach into his pocket. He dropped five dollars on the table and followed Robyn out. "Robyn."

Before Robyn got to the door she stated angrily, "Hey, don't. I accept that she got to you first, but we already knew we were starting something. I was 'that' close to sealing the deal with you. I can't believe I got beaten out by one of the oldest sluts on the planet. We need to take STD tests if we're going to stay together."

Those who spoke English in the restaurant looked up as Robyn crossed the door threshold into the light. The patrons looked at Mark as he followed her out the door.

Mark caught up and put his hand lightly on Robyn's shoulder gently turning her around. "Eirene asked about you, about us, about our future, if I wanted it. That's how I ended up back on the boat and that's why she didn't kill you, because of us, not in spite of us. She wants to give us a chance and so do I."

Robyn paused looking at Mark. She had already made her decisions and knew her feelings, no matter what. Robyn smirked and joked, "I guess it's too late for the STD tests." She grabbed Mark's arm and they walked down the street toward the bay. While walking she continued, "I'm hurt and pissed off. Just hearing that you slept with her makes me want to puke and take a shower. You need a shower too, boy toy."

16

In Port Alor, Chris managed the clean-up crew on the Eolian, swabbing the decks, cleaning cabins, checking cabinets, drawers, bedding, under mattresses, all the while looking for Raoul's data chip. He concluded the obvious. As the cleaning crew returned to shore in one skiff, Chris watched from the second deck rail as Kylie and Raoul approached in another. "Welcome aboard the Eolian, Raoul. You're alive! Kylie, greetings lover." Chris blew Kylie a kiss.

Kylie smiled back, "Hello, my love."

Raoul replied to Chris, "I'm alive. The doctors got the infection under control with a stack of antibiotics. They don't know what the infection is so they sent it off to a virologist or someone for further analysis. I'm able to move around but no diving for a while. I have to return to the clinic for new dressings every two days until my skin heals and seals."

"I guess we're not shaking hands," jested Chris. "I packed up your stuff as best I could but you might want to check it over and make some adjustments. Do you have time for a beer?"

Kylie announced, "Yep, we have time. Top deck?"

"I'll get the beer." Chris walked into the galley and grabbed three beers out of the refrigerator and made his way up the switchback stairwell to the top deck and sat at the central table. He opened his beer while listening to Raoul go through his gear on the dive deck. Chris knew there was money in any video clip of a new species that might be on Raoul's computer and Chris wanted to see it and show Kylie.

Kylie and Raoul came up and sat down as Chris slid them their beers and announced, "Cheers to a crazy recovery, Raoul. Glad you made it through."

Raoul nodded in gratitude, "Thanks. Yeah, I just remember getting bit, passing out, waking up in my bed, and talking to Sophie and Caroline then you guys."

Kylie explained, "I want to get to the point. What do you remember of the dive and what you think you saw? Something is missing and we are hoping you can help identify it."

Raoul's eyes lit up and he pointed at the deck, "There's an undiscovered species down there. I swear."

Chris looked at Kylie's expression of disbelief and asked, "From our first dive, you took video and looked at it on your computer, yes? Does any of this make sense?"

Raoul shrugged and said, "All of it. I didn't lose my mind. I got bitten, fell asleep for a couple days, and got an infection from an animal I can't identify."

Kylie thought about it and asked, "So Chris, Sari, and Sophie saw a different video with a woman watching from behind rocks. Raoul, you were unconscious and didn't see her but your video did. And Chris, you think she's real along with the animal that bit Raoul?"

Chris nodded and said, "I do. And I have Sari and Sophie to back up my story. Raoul raised his bandaged right arm as best he could and announced, "There is a creature down there.

That, I know. I never had a chance to see the video with a woman in it."

Chris looked at Raoul and said, "As I recall, you downloaded the first clip on your computer. After you got bit, we looked at your camera chip and now we can't find it. All we have is your first video."

Raoul looked at Kylie and Chris and said, "The first clip is downloaded on my computer. I'll go get it." Raoul got up.

Chris put out his arm toward Kylie and explained to Raoul, "Kylie wants proof of what we saw. Can you prove it, please? I'll go get more beer." Chris got up to go downstairs.

Kylie asked Chris as he was leaving, "Do we have the GPS tag on the site?"

"Yep. I had one of the skiff drivers enter it in when we dropped the tanks. Just wait for the video." Chris left the deck.

Kylie sat thinking of the possibilities of such a find. She looked at her phone and found the schedule and destinations for the upcoming expeditions. The rest of the season concentrated on diving out of Labuan Bajo to Rinca and Komodo Islands, the most western town on Flores Island. There was no way to get back to the site any time soon.

Chris and Raoul came up separate stairwells. Chris put down the beer and Raoul opened his computer.

Kylie questioned, "Hypothetically, let's say this woman is down there. And let's assume the marine animal you saw, that bit Raoul, is somehow connected. Not many experienced divers dive there due to the unpredictable current, as we learned. It's a perfect place for someone to live at great depth without being approached. Now, I'm guessing you want to go back and check it out some day?"

Chris nodded, "Yeah, if possible. Think of it; first contact."

Kylie asked, "Don't you think that may have already occurred with Mark? He was conveniently unconscious or forgot that part."

Raoul interrupted, "I've got it here."

Kylie and Chris rounded the table and stood behind Raoul to watch the clip. As they watched, Kylie looked for irrefutable evidence that this was a new species.

Raoul pointed at the screen and slowed it down frame to frame, "And here it comes. There, look. Four legs." He froze the screen.

Kylie nodded, "I see what you're seeing. There is something there with four legs, but that could be anything. It could be a saltwater crocodile from that frame or any other you've shown me. All you have is a silhouette of a black shadow against deep blue. We need real proof." She could see on their faces they were trying to figure out options. Kylie continued, "We have no more trips going that way this season. And for you, Raoul, due to the extent of your injuries and time not diving, we will have to wait until next year or maybe more before we can get this expedition together. The alternative is - we leave her and the creature alone and be content with the thought that there are still secrets in this world and she or they are one of them. Just think about it."

Chris cracked a beer and explained, "Let's go make some money and then plan this out. I'll be right back."

Kylie looked out the bay and watched a small pod of dolphins play in a bow wake of an outbound vessel. The dolphins took turns charging out of the water and racing along side by side. Kylie tried to put it all in perspective.

"Considering you were bitten and Chris says a woman was watching is a pretty sure sign she doesn't like visitors. I'm not saying don't go, but I'm thinking one of you might get bitten again, or both of you, so we have to prepare for the worst. We need to get enough bandages for more injuries and the antibiotics that go with those hypothetical injuries."

Raoul nodded and agreed, "I'll pick up dressings and antibiotics during my next few visits and we can store them with you, Kylie."

Kylie nodded and said, "Yep, that's fine. Chris and I will be here diving or something while waiting for you to get back then we can go check it out. And when you get new bandages at the clinic, watch how they prepare you and dress the wounds. We can get all we need at the clinic, pharmacy, or pick it up somewhere else. We can't go without them."

Chris came up the stairs with six beers, stowed them in the freezer and suggested, "We could take spear guns."

Kylie's mouth dropped open, she looked at Chris as if he was daft, "Are you not listening? Raoul was bitten last time and you say a woman was watching. Now you want to rock up with weapons? How do you expect her to react, and this being your second encounter? You'll both be killed. You are choosing to investigate something on your own accord. You better think this through."

"Yeah, good point," stated Chris.

"Understood. We have time," replied Raoul.

Kylie thought for a moment before commenting, "Now it's only you two setting out to find the unbelievable and prove your claims. We cannot talk about this to anyone." Kylie raised her glass to the others, "Here's to one of the greatest discoveries in centuries."

17

FIVE YEARS LATER

In San Francisco, rain pelted the night, drains overflowed and brown water boiled out of manhole covers. Mark was recording new book arrivals in a ledger and duplicating the information in a computer folder. He put the books in a cart and placed them in their appropriate category alphabetically. As he moved toward the front of the store, Mark looked up and saw a child standing under the street lamp in the rain on the opposite side of the road staring back at him. Mark stopped briefly to put up another book. When he looked back the child was gone. Mark went to the front window and searched the street briefly before returning to his books and shelves. It was closing time and after the till had been counted and put in the safe, Mark began turning out lights except one over the counter, where he had a small stack of various mythology books. A car horn sounded outside and Mark turned off the last light, locked the door behind him and got in Robyn's car.

Robyn chirped, "Hey."

Mark smiled and said, "Hey, you. What a day. The rain hasn't let up."

Robyn agreed, "I know. In the financial district, you need a canoe and a stick to get around. It's been reduced to waterways all heading for the bay. Sub-basements and below ground parking are pumping out water as fast as the rain is pouring in. Crazy. Where to?"

"In this weather? I think home is best," suggested Mark. He looked over his shoulder back to the street lamp and saw nothing but silver rain drops flashing through the cone of light.

Robyn noticed Mark looking back and she glanced in her rearview mirror before asking, "What's up?"

Mark turned forward and looked at Robyn, "I don't know. Something strange just happened before you showed up. There was a child standing by itself under the light across the street in the pouring rain. The next time I looked, it was gone. Then you arrived a few minutes later."

"It?" Was it a boy or a girl?"

"No idea. It was dark and raining. There was rain on the outside and condensation on the inside of the window. I couldn't see clearly," replied Mark and added, "But I got a feeling."

Robyn waited impatiently. "Dude, I am going to grow old waiting for you to finish a thought."

Mark took a deep breath before he answered, "I think it's one of Eirene's kids."

Robyn teased, "Hello. A child from Eirene is probably one of yours."

Mark looked at Robyn, "Yep."

"Tell you what. I'll come join you tomorrow afternoon at the store. I'll pick up lunch and help you around the shop while we wait and see what happens."

Mark smiled and added, "That would be great because there's a big new order coming in tomorrow. You can help me with the heavy lifting. Oh, and I have your birthday present."

101

Robyn drove past the corner of Haight and Ashbury Streets and started looking for parking. "Don't change the subject. My birthday isn't for two months. How big is it?"

Mark teased, "Bigger than a bread box."

"Where is this bread box?"

"It comes in the shipment tomorrow." Mark watched a car turn on its lights, its blinker, and start to pull out. "There's a spot."

Robyn slowed the car to a crawl and glanced over to their front staircase. A person in a heavy raincoat sat on the stairs. "We have a visitor." Robyn nodded toward their stairs as she parked.

Mark looked over and said, "At least it's not another child."

"Speaking of which, after we get married, am I going to be the stepmother to a bunch of fish?" Robyn chuckled and turned off the engine and reached into the backseat for her bag.

Mark laughed, "After we get married?"

With Robyn's hand on the door handle she explained, "Next weekend. I already bought the airline tickets, reserved the preacher and paid for the room."

"Where?"

"Vegas, Baby. We don't have to make a big deal of it. Just go get hitched, consummate our marriage for a long while, then go party. You're going to need some spending money or win big because I'm not eating fast food ever again, but I will accept a kaleidoscope and a lifelong commitment from you to be my ball and chain."

Mark stroked his chin exaggerating thought, "Wow, such choices. Both end with me being your ball and chain. Isn't it supposed to be the other way around? You're supposed to be my ball and chain."

Robyn got out of the car and exaggerated, "Oh, please."

Mark got out of the car and Robyn auto-locked the doors. They began to walk across the street to their house. Robyn asked, "So?"

Mark put his arm over Robyn's shoulders and hugged her affectionately and replied, "Kaleidoscope, huh. I might be able to manage. I can probably find one at an antique shop or on eBay."

"Okay, as your fiancé, I'm going to have Brooks Brothers make you a suit. We can get you fitted tomorrow."

Amazed at the speed Robyn jumped to the task, Mark asked, "Did you plan this all out, or have you done this before? Like a black widow scenario, eventually killing the husband and leaving everything to the wife?"

"Oh, you don't have to worry about that. You don't have anything." Robyn laughed. "Now, let's see who our guest is. Or maybe they just need a dry doorway."

As Mark and Robyn approached, the figure on the stairs stood up and pulled back her hood. Shocked, Mark and Robyn stopped in their tracks. Robyn stepped out from under Mark's arm and walked forward slowly. "Kylie?"

Kylie and Robyn hugged.

Mark came forward and greeted Kylie, "It's great to see you. It's been what, four- five years?"

Kylie nodded sheepishly and said, "Yeah, good to see you both too. Yeah, it's been five years."

Robyn looked at Kylie and felt something wasn't right and asked, "Please come in and join us for dinner, or the night if you haven't made any arrangements."

Kylie confessed, "I don't have anything planned and I would love to come in and join you for dinner and the night."

Robyn pulled out her keys and pointed down the street talking to Mark, "Can you go get a couple bottles of red and white and beer for you. I'm going to get Kylie to the shower, put her clothes in the washer, and give her some of ours to wear. A little girl time would be appreciated. How about thirty minutes? Maybe go to the local for one or two. I'll take care of dinner. See you in a bit, love you." Robyn kissed Mark on the lips, looked into his eyes, smiling. Robyn turned and took Kylie by the arm and went inside the house.

Mark stood on his doorstep for a moment looking at his closed door. He turned toward the torrent of rain running down the street. He put up his hood and headed down to the corner store and neighborhood pub. He stepped into the shop and found two Merlots and two Chardonnays. He wandered along the queue of refrigerator doors looking for a six-pack of Sierra Nevada Pale Ale and moved to the counter to pay, and he asked, "Hey, can I leave this here for thirty minutes or so? I'm just going next door for a couple, then I'll come pick it up. I live just there." Mark pointed up the road.

The clerk agreed, "I know where you live. Sure. I'll put the beer back in the cooler."

Mark smiled and suggested, "Thanks. Can we just put the whole bag in the cooler?"

"Sure. See you in a bit." The clerk walked off with Mark's bag and stowed it in the walk-in refrigerator while Mark walked out the door and into the pub.

The bar was dark with only a few patrons scattered about and a man and woman played pool in the back. Mark went to the bar and greeted the bartender. "Hey Gray, how's it going?"

"Good, Mark. Beer?"

"Yes, please. Man this rain is epic."

Gray poured a pint of IPA from a tap and agreed, "Tell me about it. I've mopped this floor every hour since eleven o'clock this morning. You could eat off it by now, ceviche or gazpacho anyway." The bartender smiled as he walked Mark's beer over and set it in front of him.

Mark raised his beer and replied, "I'll take your word for it. I'm not really a cold soup kind of guy. Cheers."

"How are the bookworms treating you?"

"It's slow with the rain but I don't mind. I get to do some research and order the books I want to read and then sell later."

Gray got another whiskey for a shadow of a man sitting at the far end of the bar, stuck to the stool like a barnacle to a ship's hull. Gray asked Mark, "Just curious Mark, what are you researching? Here you go, sir. Gray set a scotch and water in front of the elder."

"Mythology mostly. I'm trying to figure out the lineage of mythological creatures and gods' names. It appears that some names change over time and I'm trying to chronologically line them up to understand the transition, if any."

Gray walked around the bar heading for other customers and announced, "I got a C in mythology at college. I think that was my nap class." He picked up empty beer bottles and took orders for more of the same.

As Gray returned, Mark said, "Yeah, I wasn't interested in mythology until a few years ago. Pretty creative stories, whether you believe in that stuff or not."

Gray put the empties in their perspective recycling crates and prepared the new orders. "What else is going on in your life?"

Mark drank his beer and looked at himself in the mirror behind the bar and said, "I think I just got engaged."

Some people within earshot started giggling as Gray placed new beers and cocktails down in front of various patrons before returning to the bar. Gray looked at Mark and explained, "That's not really an 'I think' kind of moment. Either you are or you aren't."

Mark nodded, "I am engaged."

"Then congratulations. Next beer is on the house." Gray came to Mark and shook his hand then began pouring another beer. As he brought it over, he looked out the window and tilted his head for Mark's attention and said, "You don't see that every evening."

Mark looked at Gray and then out the window and saw four children standing in the rain across the street. He knew who they were. He swilled his first beer and pushed the empty over to Gray. "I'll be right back."

"Sure." Gray wiped around where Mark had been seated and watched him walk out into the rain.

Mark put his hood up while staring at the children. He walked over and greeted them, "Hello. Are you okay?" Mark knelt down, eye to eye.

The children all nodded and giggled together.

Mark smiled back at them and asked, "Are we related, I feel like I know you."

The children giggled and pushed each other back and forth until one child stepped forward and replied, "Yes, we are and yes, you are."

Amazed Mark asked, "How did you find me?"

Another child pointed to the gutter and blurted, "You're in the water."

Mark pointed to himself and asked, "I'm in the water?"

The first child and the tallest explained, "Your scent is in the water."

"Oh. Maybe I need a shower." Mark chuckled quietly.

"It won't help. Everybody has a scent."

"This weather is really nasty. Do you want to come inside where it's dry and warm?"

The children simultaneously shook their heads and the child in front of Mark explained, "We can't go inside. We need the rain in order to come on land, otherwise we have to stay in the rivers or ocean."

"But this is fresh water."

"One of our grandfathers was a river god so we are able to be in both fresh and salt water, and this water here is not fresh," stated the child. "We wanted to meet you and ask you a question."

"Oh? I wanted to meet you too. What's the question?"

One child explained, "We had an intruder. They took something. Mom says the woman was on the boat with you five years ago and three of them came back recently. The divers were dealt with by mother and the dragon, but the woman snuck in another way and stole something. Mom brought it back but she wants the woman. The woman is at your house now. Can you kill her?"

Mark looked at the ground and then shook his head, "That's not possible. I will go to prison and I won't be able to see you for many years. That's not how we work on land. I'm sorry."

The child looked confused and asked slowly, "On land, isn't it legal to have war and kill many people?"

"Not legal, but it happens that way, yes."

"So war murder is okay but killing one person is not legal?"

Mark sadly nodded and replied, "Something like that. There is always war. It's confusing to us too. War is caused by a difference in beliefs, greed, power over others and or their resources. It's never for the people, unless it's their own land being invaded."

The children nodded and clicked amongst themselves before one child replied, "We will tell mother. She wants to talk to you and Land-ma anyway."

Puzzled, Mark repeated, "Land-ma?"

"Robyn is our land mother because she takes care of you. When are you getting married?"

Mark was surprised at their awareness and responded, "This weekend, I think."

They all laughed and one questioned, "You think?"

Mark clarified, "Yes, I am getting married to Robyn this weekend. It just hasn't sunk in yet. I think I'm in shock meeting you all, and Robyn's directness."

The children tapped on each other's shoulders before walking toward the bay. One child remained. "The rain is going to stop for a little while. We have to stay wet. Say hello to Land-ma for us." The child walked off after his brothers and sister.

Mark stood in dismay with a grin on his face watching the children walk off into the night. Rain had soaked through the lining of Mark's coat and a chill ran down his back. He returned to the bar and put his jacket over the back of his chair to drip dry.

Gray looked at Mark and asked, "They okay?"

Mark grabbed his beer. "Thanks for the beer. Yeah, they're good. They just got a little off track. They're sorted." Mark knew it was time to get moving. He dropped some money on the bar, took another swig of beer, and looked out the window, trying to figure out where he fit into this puzzle besides siring fish. He thought of what he would tell Robyn and smiled.

Gray came over and took the money off the bar and made change. He brought it back and laid it on the table. "Congratulations on your engagement."

"Thanks. We'll come by and celebrate with some friends when it's all ball and chained." Mark waved languidly at Gray and the others before walking out toward the liquor store. The rain had backed off to a sprinkle and he thought of the child's accurate and timely prediction. He picked up his bag at the store and went up the street to his door and rang the bell even though he had keys. Mark could hear someone bouncing down the stairs to the door.

Robyn opened the door knowingly. "Hey. Sorry about that exit but it was necessary. I'm so sorry. I just wanted to apologize before it stewed in your head for no apparent reason. What'd you get?"

Walking in the door and heading for the stairs, Mark glanced at the bag. "Two Merlots, two Chardonnays and a six-pack of Sierra. Everything okay here with Kylie?"

"She has a story to tell but she's insisting you be present so she would only have to say it once. Dinner is almost ready."

The doorbell rang behind them.

Mark handed the wine bag to Robyn and went for the door. It was the pizza guy with two large pizzas. Mark looked snidely up the stairs to see Robyn looking back with a grin. He turned and looked at the pizza guy. "Hi. How much?"

"Good evening. That'll be thirty-two bucks."

Mark handed him thirty-five and said, "Thanks. Help your family." Mark took the pizza boxes with a smile, closed the door and headed up the stairs. He walked into the kitchen and put the boxes in the oven to stay warm.

Robyn handed him a beer. "The rest are in the fridge and the red is warming. Just FYI, red wine needs to be room temperature in order for it to breathe properly. How's the local?"

Mark took off his wet jacket and hung it on a hook on the back of the door leading to the bathroom and their bedroom to the left. He moved back into the kitchen, had a sip of beer, and leaned against a countertop, "Yeah, pretty good. Six or so people plus me. Gray's in. I told him we'd have a gathering at the bar after Vegas."

"You told him?"

"Yep, and he bought me a beer."

Robyn smiled, "Okay, so we're having a party there?"

"Sounds good." Mark put a finger to his lips and spoke quietly, "And four kids showed up." Mark looked out the door into the living room. "Where's Kylie?"

"Changing into stuff in our room." Robyn crossed her arms and asked, "So does that make five so far or four?"

Mark smirked. "I think five. They said to say hello to 'Land-ma.' That's what they call you."

Robyn poured a cold glass of Merlot and quaffed it. She smiled and put up a finger in gest, "I've been called a lot of things but, Land-ma?"

"They're five years old, but mentally going on thirty. Smart, clever, and curious about us. I told them we're getting married this weekend and they told me Eirene wants to talk to us when we get back. Unfortunately, they know Kylie is here and Eirene isn't happy."

Robyn rasped quietly, "Oh, now you're telling everyone we're getting married and you want me to meet up with your nymphomaniac cradle-robbing cougar tart again?"

Mark laughed and pointed at Robyn, "You're the one that told me she wanted to see you again. Didn't she say, she'd give back your fertility or something?"

"Why? You need the Guinness Book of World Records for most offspring? I'm good with that. But, she's entering a competition. I want to be pregnant every year until I run out of eggs."

Laughing, Mark hugged Robyn, "Done."

Robyn felt calmed in Mark's arms and added, "Practice makes perfect. Robyn felt his warmth and security from within and added, "I'm still coming with you tomorrow."

"Good. You'll be there for your birthday present."

"Thank you for thinking of me. But, I also want another present on my birthday."

"It'll be a kaleidoscope."

Robyn smiled and replied, "Promises, promises."

Mark and Robyn's bedroom door opened and Kylie walked down the hall and into the kitchen wearing Robyn's pajama bottoms and a sweatshirt from Mark. "Hey, I hope you don't mind. This is the most comfortable combination I found."

Mark waved her off, "No worries. Get what you need. I'm off for a hot shower and out of these wet clothes." Mark walked down the hall to the bedroom.

Robyn reached for a wine glass and asked, "White or red?"

"White, please." Kylie continued, "Thanks so much for your hospitality. It's been a while since I've felt secure and relaxed. I've been looking for you two, then I remembered what Chris said about ways to find you through Facebook, Instagram, email addresses from expedition records, and listed phone numbers."

"Glad to have you. Plus, I want to hear about your scuba diving adventures. We miss it. We don't really go anymore. Mark says California water is often too murky and cold compared to South East Asia. He's spoiled and a little timid about entering the ocean these days." Robyn handed Kylie her glass of Chardonnay with a gracious knowing smile.

Kylie smelled her wine and put it on the table and asked, "So, how and what have you guys been doing?"

Robyn nodded confidently and replied, "We're good. Working mostly. I've been working for the same architectural engineering firm since we got back from Indonesia and Mark took over my uncle's bookshop while he is going through a midlife crisis and romancing his way across Europe. Mark was supposed to manage the store for one year, but here we are five years later. Let's move into the living room. I ordered one vegetarian and one pepperoni pizza. I don't remember you being particular."

"I'm not particular. Sounds great." Kylie grabbed a pillow and put it in the bend of her knee. She watched Robyn get comfortable and then asked, "So you're not diving?"

"We really haven't had much time. Our holidays don't exactly line up. Mark eventually trained a woman to run the store but, she has a regular job five days a week. She's a single mom with two kids and family nearby to take the kids when need be. I'm more on a schedule, weekends off, some holiday time around Easter and Christmas. You know, the usual Christian holidays." Robyn shrugged her shoulders.

Kylie was curious and asked, "I take it you're not much of a church goer?"

Robyn shook her head and calmly replied, "Church goer, no. Things happened when I was a kid. I went to catechism with all the other children but there was a problem with a priest and he was transferred. My parents never allowed me to go back. Over time, I lost sight of the contemporary human interpretations, but that doesn't mean I don't believe there may be something out there. Considering the age of the planet, I doubt whatever it is has human form, just saying. It's like, all the religions we've destroyed throughout history, even the Crusades. Both sides had their beliefs and they thought they were right and fought for it, correct or not, still do. Christians and Muslims have invested too much time and study in belief, faith and influence to back down now. That's why Darwinism was so blasphemous; it had merit and yet, could not be accepted because it wasn't by the hand of God. Look at places like Bali today; Island of the Gods they call it. Outsiders don't understand Balinese Gods but Islanders' are devout in their beliefs. The Balinese religion is an evolution of interpretation of Hinduism. Bali has Muslims, Christians, Hindu, a heap of other religions, plus spirits, ghosts, and the locals believe and make daily offerings. It's not my place to put a name on it. I'd say there is something, but not written or understood by humans. We are all still so ignorant. A great example is when the Europeans, British, and North Americans killed thousands of women accused of witchcraft, innocent women, all because they didn't have an answer for the great plague or some other unseen disease. American Indians, Latin Americans, Aboriginals in Australia, plus numerous other cultures believe in Mother Nature—the Sun, the Moon and the stars—and they lived with their beliefs daily and respected life. How many cultures did we eradicate? Today, people still experience war, slavery, forced prostitution, kidnappings, mafias, money laundering, poverty, starvation, uncontrollable toxic waste, pollution, over-population, lack of sanitation and drinkable water, and those in power have put greed above all else, including the church. No one and no-thing is coming to save us. No, I don't have faith, especially not in humans. The Earth will be here long after we are gone and will heal itself without us. Can you imagine what would happen if someone proved that there are no gods? Wow."

Kylie tried to steer the conversation, "Maybe like the Greeks, Romans, or Middle Eastern cultures that took over parts of the world and had their own gods with different names and influenced weaker cultures by flexing their military arm. Conquerors were seen as powerful and intelligent, and religious conversions followed, like that?"

"I guess so. Yeah. Obviously, there is no definitive answer to the existence of a god or gods. They are mostly built on a cocktail of faith, fear and hallucinogens. We should be able to choose, not be brainwashed or forced into belief. It's one of the main reasons people fled England and Europe for the Americas in the first place ... for freedom of religion and from religious and cultural persecution. For having a difference of opinion, free thinking, and not shunned for it. Plus, escaping war for a better life is always a good reason to flee. The problem is, again, believing in the wrong religion in the wrong place is a crime and we're running out of places to run for safety. Too many rats in a cage type thing."

Mark poked his head around the hallway corner shirtless and drying his hair with a towel, "Sorry to interrupt. Like Kylie said, when the Romans took over Europe, Greece for example, the Romans had their gods which, at the time, became common practice, and the Greek gods became myth and legend, but maybe they are still the same gods, like how Poseidon became Neptune. I've been reading up on this stuff at the shop and there's some support for it. I didn't want to miss the conversation. Sorry. I can hear you. Keep talking." Mark disappeared down the hall.

Kylie nodded. "Agreed. I just have one more question to ask. Did you guys meet the woman in Indonesia?"

Mark froze in the hall and waited in suspense for Robyn's reply.

Robyn knew immediately what Kylie was fishing for. "Who?"

Kylie put her glass on the table. "The woman under water. Did you meet her?"

Robyn shook her head, "No. What woman?"

Kylie picked up her glass and looked at Robyn. "It's really weird, because, apparently, she kills everyone that she comes in contact with, especially women. I contacted Sophie who knows South East Asian history and folklore. We did some research on the legends in the area and something or someone has been in that channel through the ages."

Robyn raised her eyebrows. "Kylie, I don't know what you're talking about."

Kylie pointed at Robyn, "That night or late afternoon, when you went to your room because you didn't want to hear the outcome of our choice to save Raoul or stay with the rescue for Mark. You must have interrupted her. You met her and she let you live. Why?"

Robyn wondered how much Kylie knew and asked, "On the boat? Why do you think I met someone? That doesn't make sense."

Kylie got up to get more wine, stalling, waiting for Mark to return.

Mark walked into the kitchen, grabbed another beer and sat next to Robyn in the living room.

After pouring another glass, Kylie stood in the middle of the room, in front of Mark and Robyn and began, "Okay, so when Mark, Pierre, Caroline and Chris dived the first time, they didn't see anything strange but the current took you down. Right?" Kylie looked at Mark.

Mark nodded.

Kylie continued, "Chris and the others lost sight of you over the wall. They got caught in an up draft and popped up near the shore. You still went down." Again, looking at Mark for confirmation.

Mark nodded and replied, "Yeah, then I fought for a while, grabbed the rocks, lost my hold and passed out on the way down."

Kylie continued, "Right. Then, later, Chris and Raoul went down and dropped two tanks for you. While they did that, a strange creature showed up. Raoul videoed it. The second time they went down to retrieve the tanks, Raoul got bit by the same creature."

Robyn shook her head pretending to be confused, "Is that the data card you asked me about that night? I thought that card disappeared?"

"It did, but Raoul had downloaded the first dive video on his computer before the data card disappeared. There was definitely something strange going on. Plus, all three tanks were back on board, Mark's and the two extra tanks. Well, after Raoul was treated and released, we wanted to go back and dive it again. We saved our money for a couple years and went back. We found nothing. No evidence of any kind. No creature and no woman. Nothing."

Mark asked calmly, "You went back? Why would you do that? It's a dangerous dive site. There should be a divers warning on that site."

Staying with the subject, Kylie replied, "Because Chris, Sophie, and Sari all swear they saw a woman down there and Chris and Raoul wanted proof. We all would have been rich with such a find. I agreed to go with them, but not to dive. I warned them she may not want to be found. They disregarded my warning and Raoul and Chris dove. We didn't see her. It continued to bug Chris and one day he called Raoul in Buenos Aires and talked about it. Six weeks ago we went back for one last look. She and her pet were waiting. She went after the boys. I chose a different path. Through binoculars, I caught sight of a child on the beach and I took a skiff over while the others were diving. I followed some footprints and found a hidden entrance and went in." Kylie looked frightened and paused before confessing, "I took something."

Mark and Robyn looked at each other and Mark asked, "What did you take?"

Kylie laughed at herself, "I don't know. It was encased in barnacles, dead coral, and corrosion. I know it's old. I haven't had the time, the place, or the means to check it out. Anyway, Chris and Raoul dived side mount, two tanks each." Kylie paused in a saddened state and quietly added, "Raoul died down there and I never saw Chris again. We searched for three hours. Between what I knew and the captain and crew's superstitions of the area, we didn't stick around like we did for you, Mark. We couldn't. We recovered Raoul's body and

Chris remains missing. We could only presume the worst. Chris had been my partner for eight years and I had to abandon him."

"Kylie, I'm so sorry. Chris and Raoul were good people and great divers." Mark waited for the solemn moment before leaning forward intently, "You pulled Raoul's body out of the water?"

Wiping away tears, Kylie replied, "Yes, he floated to the surface, torn to shreds with numerous stab wounds."

Robyn got up from the couch and walked toward the kitchen, "That's horrible. What a way to go." A moment passed. "I'm getting more wine and pull out the pizzas. Anybody want anything?"

Mark waited, watching Kylie. "So, you're obviously not carrying this artifact around with you. Is it in a safe place?"

Kylie shrugged. "I don't know. She may have already found it. I couldn't take it far. I certainly couldn't put it on a plane. But, if she finds me, I think she'll kill me for taking it and for knowing where she lives. Although I've never seen her or met her I now know she exists. I did something wrong and I know it now."

Robyn asked out of the kitchen, "So, why come find us? I'm glad you did, but why us, after all this time?"

"As I said before, you are the only two that lived."

Mark responded, "But we don't know any woman, especially not underwater. I'm sorry."

"Or maybe you don't remember, or you know and won't say," offered Kylie.

Mark shook his head and remarked, "That's not something I'd forget."

Kylie eyed Mark and added, "That still leaves option two."

Robyn responded, "This all sounds a little crazy to me." Robyn placed three plates on the kitchen counter, re-cut the pizza, and put some on each plate. "Pizza is hot and there's salad and dressings on the counter. Help yourselves."

18

The rain had returned with a vengeance. Hong wore a heavy Australian Oilskin trench coat and held an umbrella overhead as he walked below the Golden Gate Bridge to Fort Point. The waves crashed on the rocky shore and splashed white wash through the metal posts and chain guard separating the road from the sea. Spot lights beamed on top of the red brick fortress built before the American Civil War and originally called, Castillo de San Joaquin. Hong stopped at the end of the guardrail and watched the storm swell wrap around the shoreline.

Eirene walked up the breakwater boulders and crossed the guardrail. "Hello, old friend. How have you been?" The sea dragon remained in the water with his head raised for Hong to see.

"Hello Eirene. I'm fine. Thanks for asking. Your sea dragon has grown since I last saw it."

Eirene looked back at the edge of the bay where her ride stood on the rocks and watched. "Yeah, and he's still a baby."

"Yeah, a thousand-year-old baby sea dragon. Great." Hong looked up into the rain and continued, "You sure picked a fine evening to meet."

"You know the rules, Hong. And it's older than one thousand years, but you know that. You obviously met Mark and Robyn?"

Yes. I've spent time with Mark on numerous occasions. He's trying to figure out your history, much like I tried before but he has more resources than I did."

"How's he doing with that?"

Hong nodded and responded, "He's putting the pieces together and going back in time, way past what I could figure out. He's smart, even though Robyn wears the pants, as they say."

"How far back has he gone?"

"He's well past the Greeks and Egyptians. He knows things about you I never would have considered."

"How's he dealing with it?"

"He's keeping it to himself. He doesn't even tell Robyn what he has discovered besides the blatant truths she would need to know as a partner."

Eirene raised her eyebrows, "So Robyn knows about Mark and me. How's she dealing with that knowledge?"

"Like I said, she wears the pants, but she would follow him off the edge of the earth."

"You like her?"

Hong bowed his head. "Yes. Please don't kill this one."

"I won't. I want to kill the other one. My kids say she's at Mark and Robyn's house right now. Do you know where they live?"

"Yes, but maybe there's more to it than just killing everyone. Plus, I know you can scent her out on your own and you can always find Mark and Robyn. Why are you asking me? I feel like I'm just another pawn in your game."

Eirene shrugged her shoulders and confirmed, "You are a pawn. And, you're one of my only confidants and I need your help. You've been in touch with some of the others before and after you. I'm sure they've given you a few clues after telling their tales."

Hong confessed, "Yes, we've shared a lot of drinking and storytelling, and I found out you didn't always live in the same place, at least for some of them, and not under the same name."

"No, I didn't always live in the same place. I have many homes around the world's oceans. And I presumed you would have compared and contrasted your times with the others, like boys do. That's fine. As you have probably figured out, some have died and there will be gaps in the storyline that only I know. You certainly won't know the beginning of the journey unless I tell you."

"That's true, but still. Why are you so exposed now? I hadn't seen you in centuries and here you are twice in five years."

"I kept their friend Chris alive. He's down with dragon sleep for a while, off and on. I'll deal with him later. I need to know what he knows then I can stitch this up and put it behind me."

Hong nodded, "You're going to kill him like all the others. You really do need some social skills."

"This is not the time for socializing. My private life is unraveling and I want it boxed up. Mark and Robyn have kept their end of the bargain, like you, and I'm good with that but, these other two are meddling in something they don't understand and never will. I have to put an end to it."

Hong asked, "How can I help? What do you want me to do?"

"I need you to talk to Mark and Robyn, see what they know and find out what the woman knows. She snuck into my house from land and took something. I got it back but, still she knows too much. I have to find her and end her and all the people she told of my land entrance."

"And the other guy in your dungeon?"

"He's for the dragon. Can you get on this tonight?"

Hong bowed his head, "I thank you and owe you for my long life. I'll do what is necessary, but I'm not killing anyone."

"Talk to you soon. I have to get home before the man wakes up. I'll let you know."

"I'm sure you will." Hong turned and walked in to the dark rain.

Eirene walked back into the sea and disappeared on the back of her dragon.

19

Chris opened his eyes and listened. All he could hear was dripping water. With sand caked to his face he raised his head and looked around. He saw a limestone wall in a circular room with two opposing corridors, one sloped up and another led downward. His hands and feet were bound with a strong seaweed. He began wrestling with the bonds around his wrists. After a few minutes he figured out the knot and untied his hands, then his feet and stood up slowly. Chris moved to one of the corridors to listen intently. Not hearing anything, he began to explore the passage sloping up but only found empty rooms. The temperature was rising and Chris began to sweat in the humidity. Seeing no exit, Chris turned and crept down the passage. Passing Eirene's lavish bedroom, he continued down until he reached the underwater cave entrance. His tanks and equipment lay in the sand and he hastily put on his gear, checked his air in both tanks and made his escape. His computer showed normal signs and he entered the water and swam out into the blue and immediately began to ascend up the cliff wall watching his bubbles rise ahead of him. Fortunately for Chris, there was little current and his floatation device did most of the work as he tried to conserve his air consumption knowing he was instantly at 80 meters and there would be one or two decompression stops before finally surfacing. He didn't know what to expect but he didn't see the woman or the strange creature.

Chris surfaced in the midday sun with little air remaining. He swam to the atoll and climbed up the beach. He dropped his BCD and tanks in the tall grass and surveyed his surroundings. There were two fishing boats in the distance, too far away to communicate and he saw no way of getting off the atoll. Driftwood and plastic garbage littered the tide line. Chris knew he had to get as far away as quickly as possible and chose to swim for the fishing boats. He knew if he missed them, that she would find him and kill him. He took his mask and fins back into the water and began to swim, periodically looking up to make sure he was on course for the boats.

An hour swimming and growing tired, Chris heard a two stroke engine banging away and getting louder. He stopped swimming and looked up to see a fishing boat bearing down on him. It slowed as it approached and a deckhand reached out to help Chris on board. He took off his fins and mask and in his broken Indonesian asked for water. He was dehydrated and exhausted. The effects of the dragon remained and he passed out.

Just after sunset, Chris woke up in a thatch hut with a lone candle for light. He could smell the fishing village before he could see it. He got up and went to the doorway. He saw a small fire in a clearing with a group of people close by. He could see a woman flipping fish on the flat stones surrounding the fire and she looked up and saw Chris looking back at her. He watched her speak to the others. The children all stopped playing and turned their heads toward Chris.

Chris vaguely recognized one of the fishermen walking toward him with a young girl. As they approached, the young girl spoke, "Salamat Malam. Good evening. Are you feeling better?"

Chris stepped out from under the thatch eave, "Yes. Thank you. You speak English?"

"I speak some English I learned in school. My father invites you to join us by the fire and have some food. Please." The girl and the fisherman led the way.

Chris put his hands together and bowed his head slightly. "Thank you. That is very kind." Chris followed the pair back to the fire.

A woman came forward carrying a plastic chair and looked at Chris.

As Chris sat down, all the little children ran to their mothers and grabbed hold of their dresses to shyly watch Chris from behind.

The fisherman and the young girl sat next to Chris and the girl introduced herself, "My name is Komong and this is my father, Kadek. He pulled you out of the sea. His older brother, Wayan, saw you and drove the boat to help you."

"Hello, my name is Chris. Please thank your father and his brother for saving me. I would have died."

Komong translated to her father and uncle. The father and uncle nodded.

Uncle Wayan asked Komong to ask Chris a question.

Komong looked at Chris and asked, "Where is your ship and crew?"

Chris flashed through the images of Raoul being attacked and repeatedly bitten by the sea creature, bleeding profusely while fighting it off. The woman stabbing Raoul through the chest, over and over again, killing him as he floated to the surface. The creature pinning Chris's arms and dragging him into a crevasse, the woman removing his mask and regulator, putting something on his face, then waking up in a labyrinth. Chris shook his head and lied, "I think the ship took the injured to the closest clinic or hospital. We will never dive there again. It's not safe."

Komong translated to all the people listening around the fire. They spoke quietly amongst themselves for a few minutes before Komong's father, Kadek, spoke to her quietly. The adults all nodded and looked at each other for confirmation.

An elderly gentleman who had been listening hobbled over to Komong and her father. The old man put his hand on Kadek's shoulder for support and sat down and began talking slowly so Komong could translate as best she could. Komong introduced the man as he sat down. "This is Made. He is the chief of our village. He grew up with my great grandfather. He was a fisherman when he was young but his father disappeared near where they found you. Our village has been here for a very long time, back to the Moken people, the sea gypsies from the West. The Moken people come from an area now called the Andaman Sea and the Bay of Bengal. The Moken people are ancient seafarers who used the stars to guide their boats they lived on; husband, wife and children, not going to land except to scavenge. They migrated the seas, following the fish. They have stories and legends of certain places where good and evil spirits live. The place they found you is one of legends. He says, if you come in good spirit, you go in good spirit. If you come with bad spirit, you don't come back at all. Another village lost two fishermen trying to net a mystical creature that our stories say lives there. Made stopped fishing and his family has been harvesting coconuts and making Arak, our local alcohol, ever since. He says it keeps him alive because fishing in these waters will not. He's the oldest and wisest man in our village and doesn't talk about his past anymore and we don't ask out of respect. He tells us what we need to know and no more."

Chris smiled at the old man and then at Komong, "Arak, huh? I'd like to try your local brew, if I may."

Komong asked her father and he got up and went and picked up a small plastic water bottle refilled with Arak and handed it to Chris. Chris took a healthy gulp and coughed abruptly at the brew's strength. Chris rasped, "Wow." He shook his head and tried again.

The villagers giggled and smiled as all tensions drifted away in the wood smoke and sea breeze.

Komong explained, "I am being taken back to a bigger town for school tomorrow. Maybe you should come with me. They have ATMs, shops, boat taxis, phone, whatever you need to help you get home. Made thinks you should go away from this place. You might be in danger or bring danger here."

Chris nodded his head and connected knowingly with the old man's eyes, "Roger that. I would really appreciate the ride."

A woman came over with two heaping plates of fish and rice and handed one to Made and the other to Chris. The rest of the villagers wandered off to get dinner, and then returned to eat and talk.

20

Late in the afternoon, Robyn was in the bookstore organizing designated spaces for the new book arrivals. Mark was upstairs clearing a central space and transferring books to the appropriate shelves on either side when the delivery truck pulled up.

Mark asked Robyn, "How you doing down there?"

"Good. Almost sorted. I still need to move a few around but it can wait, right?"

Mark smiled and responded, "Why, you looking forward to going through more books?"

"Not really. More interested in my birthday present, thank you very much."

Mark came downstairs. "Alright, let's get to it."

The door jingled and a delivery man walked in backwards pulling a dolly of stacked boxes. He stopped in front of the cashier desk and slipped the dolly out from under the boxes. "Hey Mark. Here's one of three."

The delivery man dropped off the other two stacks of boxes and put the invoice on the counter. Mark went around his counter, double-checked the books and the prices against his own, and signed the invoice. "Thanks for the timely delivery."

"Yeah, I'll see you next time around."

Robyn looked at Mark and asked the delivery man, "Is there anything else being dropped off today?"

The delivery man opened the door and stopped and exaggerated, "Oh yeah, I almost forgot your birthday present. You want to help me with it, Mark?"

Robyn smiled. "Ha-ha. Very funny."

Mark went out and took an end of a large rectangular box and the two men brought it in and carried it upstairs.

Robyn followed with a quizzical look on her face as the box was placed in the clearing. Mark handed the delivery man fifty dollars and thanked him.

The delivery man turned to Robyn, "Have a happy birthday. See you guys tomorrow with the rest of it."

Mark waved goodbye and walked to the railing to watch the delivery man walk out.

"The rest of what?" Robyn circled the box with her arms crossed. There were no labels or telling trademarks on the box. She looked at Mark and asked, "What is it?"

"It's not a toaster. Open it up." Mark handed Robyn a razor knife and watched her delicately cut away at the seams and staples.

Robyn lifted the top and looked inside. She dropped the lid and looked at Mark. "This is a drafting table. You bought me a drafting table?"

"Yeah, since you're always working late, I thought maybe you could work late here with me instead of at your office. Tomorrow there's two cabinets, an overhead lamp and a computer with a couple architectural engineering applications already installed coming to complete your second station. I have enough research to do to match your hours and I get to be with you more, if you want."

Robyn smiled. "Yes. This is a great idea. I hate my office, it's so sterile. Inspiration and creativity are drained from me in that environment. I love it. Thank you."

Mark added, "And I replaced all the books up here with architectural and engineering materials. We can replace those you don't want or can order what you do want."

"This is awesome. Thank you very much. I miss being around you." Robyn continued, "With the kids showing up and now Kylie arriving, I think something is coming and I want to be with you when it does."

"That's part of the reason I did it. Plus, apparently, I'm marrying you in a couple days."

Robyn got up and came to Mark, "That's true and I'm having two rings made as we speak. I hope you like yours, I like mine. Thank you for this, Mark. I know I'll enjoy working here. Hell, I might even get something done." Robyn kissed Mark passionately.

The door chimed and in walked Hong in his Oilskin trench coat, shaking his umbrella out the open door.

Robyn looked down at Hong and said under her breath to Mark, "Speak of the devil. No matter what Hong wants, you are busy this weekend. And you still owe me a birthday present." Robyn gently coaxed Mark toward the stairs. "You go have a chat with Hong and I'll read the manual because I know you won't, and I'll end up with a garage door for a golf cart. I love you and thank you so much." Robyn waved down. "Hello, Hong."

Hong put his umbrella in a hollow brass canister and waved up to Robyn as he watched Mark come down the stairs.

Mark walked over and shook Hong's hand. "Hey, Hong. How are you?"

"I'm good, thank you. I don't mean to intrude or take you away from your tasks at hand but maybe we could go grab a beer somewhere. All three of us." Hong looked up at Robyn who was looking back down with a concerned look on her face.

Mark glanced up to Robyn and then asked Hong, "What's this about?"

Hong winced and replied, "I'd prefer talking over a beer or two. It's a delicate subject and I'd be more comfortable in a dark bar. My treat."

Robyn heard everything and started coming down the stairs and replied, "Sounds good to me. I hate reading manuals anyway. We can save that for later. Right, Hong?"

Hong nodded with a smile. "Robyn, by the time you feel old, you will have potentially read every manual printed in English and every other language in existence. Shall we? I have a taxi waiting." Hong grabbed his umbrella and opened the door to let Robyn out.

Robyn talked over her shoulder, "I am not bringing any money and I still want a six-pack stomach."

"And you shall have it." Hong scurried around the front of the taxi and told Mark, "There is no need for coats. When we are finished with our business, I'll drop you here." Looking over the roof of the taxi Hong added, "This is important and involves us all."

Mark turned the sign to "closed" and locked the door as Robyn got in the backseat and Hong got in the front. Mark followed Robyn.

The driver didn't ask where to, he just drove off. No one spoke in the taxi until Robyn recognized the street and asked, "Where are we going?"

Hong looked back over the seat and replied, "To your local bar just ahead."

Mark and Robyn looked at each other puzzled and a bit worried.

Mark asked suspiciously, "Why here?"

"I'll explain inside. Please trust me as you have since we met. Here we are."

Mark and Robyn got out and stood on the sidewalk waiting for Hong who was explaining something to the taxi driver in Ukrainian. Mark looked at Robyn and said, "I'm getting a very strong feeling."

Robyn nodded. "So am I for a change. It's too strong to ignore."

The driver nodded at Hong and pulled toward a parking meter spot surrounded in yellow tape.

Hong removed the tape, slid his credit card into the slot, and punched in a code.

Mark warned Hong, "I don't think you're allowed to do that."

Hong smiled and admitted, "I put the tape up an hour ago." He pressed the tape into a ball, pushed the bar door open with his shoulder, simultaneously throwing the yellow tape in a bin inside the entrance, and continued on without breaking stride.

Gray was working and greeted everybody. "Good evening, Hong. Oh, and you brought the engaged! I'll buy the first round for you three, but not the others back there. Jeez, they can drink. And Hong, they say it's all on you. Is that correct?"

Hong waved Gray off and continued walking hastily. "Yes, on me. All of it. Whatever they want, but they cannot buy the bar or any female companionship. That's on them."

Mark nudged Robyn to the bar where they dropped an elbow. Dismayed, Mark leaned forward and asked Gray, "You know him?"

Gray looked after Hong entering a side room with an open entryway greeting people in numerous languages. "Hong. Yeah, as long as I've worked here, he comes in with a motley group every now and again. They talk quiet until they get a few in them, then it's all laughter. How do you know him, or them?"

Robyn blurted out, "We met him five years ago. How long have you worked here, Gray?"

Gray finished pouring two pints of Sierra Nevada and brought them over, "A little over five years now. About the same time I met you guys. Congratulations on your engagement, Robyn. It's this weekend, yeah?"

Robyn looked at Mark and smiled, "Thank you and yes. We are getting out of here this weekend to get married." She raised her glass with her wedding ring to show Gray then looked at Mark and concluded, "Drink up, buttercup."

Gray grinned and said, "If you finish it, I'll buy you another."

Mark and Robyn clinked their glasses and swilled their beers easily and put the empties on the table. While Gray walked off to get two more, Robyn asked Mark, "What have we gotten ourselves into? Hong seems to know our every move."

Mark wiped his mouth and chin with a napkin and replied, "Yeah, I know but what can we do? We are in this up to our necks as it is. Let's grab free beer and figure it out as we go. I've got your back and you have mine. But I don't know if anyone else has our backs, not even Hong." Mark nodded toward the side room.

Gray came over with two beers and placed them on the counter. "Here you go. Be careful in there, and again, congratulations. I take it, you're both on Hong's tab as well?"

Robyn smiled and replied, "Thank you Gray. And yes, it's on Hong's tab. Come on Mark, let's get this over with and remember, we are busy this weekend or so help me."

Mark followed Robyn into the side room and everybody in the room stood up. They were all men from various ethnicities. They all stared at Robyn and slightly bowed.

Hong came to Mark and Robyn's side and introduced them. "Gentlemen, I would like to introduce you to Mark and Robyn."

Robyn was confused, "Hello everybody. What is this?"

Hong explained quietly, "Over time, these men have all had roughly the same experience Mark and I had with Eirene. Every one of them, except you, Robyn. Your relationship with Eirene is different and these men are curious and wanted to meet the first woman she didn't kill and we all wonder why."

Robyn looked at the faces around the room staring back at her. "You've all slept with her?"

A Frenchman blurted out, "There wasn't much sleeping."

The group erupted in laughter and nods but never took their eyes off Robyn.

Gray came in with two more chairs and everybody moved to make room. Gray looked at Hong and said, "These are the last two chairs I can manage."

A chisel-jawed man spoke with a South African accent, "Thank you, Gray. This is all of us. If you'd be so kind, we would appreciate another round."

"You got it. Just give me a minute." Gray glanced at Mark and Robyn before walking out to the other tables.

As Robyn sat down, she exclaimed, "See Mark, I told you she was a nymphomaniac." Robyn grabbed her glass as the others chuckled.

Mark smiled, drank his beer and concentrated on the faces as they began talking amongst themselves. He noticed they all spoke each other's languages as if born to them. Eventually, when inquisitive minds turned to Mark, he told his story and they all listened intently. When the stories came to an end, all eyes reverted back to Robyn and waited for her story.

All with full glasses of various alcoholic beverages, Hong stood up and called for attention. "It is time to honor the only woman who met Eirene and lived to tell the tale." Hong continued, "Also, cheers to Robyn and Mark on their engagement. They are getting married in Los Vegas this weekend with Eirene's blessings. If any of you are inclined to go there, they're going to need witnesses and who better than those who live through the ages. It will be a monumental occasion and with your permission, Robyn and Mark, we will come and make fools of ourselves once again."

Robyn nodded in acceptance and replied, "You're all welcome." The others hooted and hollered congratulations in every language never taking their eyes off Robyn.

Gray rushed in, "What is going on here?" He looked around at all the men drinking. "Oh darn. I thought there was a stripper or something." He laughed nervously. Gray stood in amazement at the scene. Empty bottles were strewn all over the tables, glasses drained, ashtrays packed with cigarette butts, cigars smoldering on the edge of the table, ashes all over everything, foreign currencies in front of most people. Two Liar's Dice cups were tipped over with five sixes showing and a large stack of bills to the side of one of the cups. Smoke filled the air. Gray didn't know what to do except follow the rules. "Gentlemen, gentlemen, please. This is California. It's almost illegal to smoke outside, let alone inside. I will be fined and lose my job."

A British man passed Gray a small stack of English pound notes and added, "Let's keep it between us, shall we. Just warn us if the bobbies are in bound."

"I have no idea what that means. The rest of the bar is livelier and crazier than ever because of all of you. How much is this in U.S. dollars and who's the lady on the front of some of these?"

The room erupted in laughter at Gray's ignorance.

The Brit chuckled. "She's water under the London bridge and down the River Thames. God bless her. It's best you just get us a bottle of everything and a case of Guinness for my Irish mate here and two pints for the American betrothal, then go away."

"You know you people are going to drink me dry tonight."

A Turkish man added, "Out of respect, maybe it's best you go help your other tables before returning."

"Right. See to my tables then, come clean this room then, bring you your order. Hong, can I take your credit card and make sure all is okay?"

The South African spoke up, "We can pay cash for tonight so you can start ordering now."

"I need a wheelbarrow for the garbage in here." Gray walked out shaking his head.

Everybody giggled or smiled.

Robyn waited for the laughter and commentary to die down before asking, "So who is the oldest or considered the first that is still alive at this table?"

Hong touched Robyn's shoulder and explained, "We will get to your question but first, we want to know what happened to you. Why you?"

Robyn felt the eyes more than saw them and didn't know where to start.

A man from Korea added, "We have all lost loved ones, wives, children, entire families, everything over time and yet you are alive in front of us. This is puzzling to the men here. Why couldn't we choose our partners? Maybe you can shed some light and help us understand."

Mark spoke up. "Eirene asked me if I had a woman. I told her Robyn was on the boat. Eirene then told me she could make the bond between Robyn and myself permanent, forever. It was part of the proposal to get me out timely or I'd be there until I gave in or she killed me. Life on the surface would have passed me by and I wasn't willing to give up the chance of a life with Robyn." Mark shrugged and added, "So I did what I had to do." Mark drained his pint.

Robyn looked over at Mark, "You're such a cheater." Robyn looked at the others around the table and explained, "You know what it came down to? I already wanted him before Eirene blackmailed him into swamp sex. Not fine, but whatever. I would say the reason she let me live was she saw a glimpse of love and hope. Something very rare or non-existent in her world. Think of her lonely existence over time. Throughout your brief encounters with her, the hussy, what kind of interaction has she experienced? She's a predator and you were all her prey. You boy toys provided a service, nothing more. And in return, you have been alive over the centuries watching the world turn and burn and burn again."

Everybody sat in somber thought.

Robyn continued, "Some of you might think you're being punished with long life watching family members grow old and die before you, regular people overpopulate, make global mistakes like war, cause pollution, and live lives of greed, self-indulgence and ignorance. You've experienced the past, you live in the present, and you have front row fucking seats for the future. Mark and I are part of that now. I can only say that Mark wanted me and I wanted him and, for a fraction of a second, Eirene felt compassion. She has never fully trusted her partners, none of you." She pointed above them all and continued, "And maybe she never trusted herself. After thousands of years, she may still be learning as a child about some emotions. For other people in your lives, I'm guessing here, but some of your girlfriends, wives, mistresses, children, maybe they see or saw something in you that you don't see or feel yourself, or you want so badly, you can't see it, feel it, or recognize it. I'm telling you, you already have it. It was timing for us. Eirene knew how Mark felt about me and I confessed the same to her about Mark that day on the boat. There's a reason she gave you long life, we just don't know what it is." Robyn looked at Mark and added, "Maybe we can help shed light. I ask myself and you; to what end?" Robyn drained her beer and then exclaimed, "The bitch took my fertility away! She told me she'd give it back the next time I see her if I never mention her existence, and I haven't."

Gray came in with a crate of bottles and set it on a side table and started passing them out. "The rest is coming."

One of the men announced, "Double the round, please."

"Already? What is wrong with you people? You don't even seem drunk. I'd be on the floor by now."

Mark smirked, "Yeah, slurping up gazpacho."

"Ha, ha, very funny. Be right back with four beers and double cocktails." Gray then asked, "Hey Irish, do you want another case of Guinness?"

Irish explained, "Are you aware this Guinness export tastes like piss compared to true Irish Guinness from Ireland?"

As Gray walked out the entrance he offered, "Last chance, Irish."

"Oh, yes please. Thank you, Gray. You're an honorable mixed blood."

Robyn still held court. "Did that help quench your curiosity? I know the booze isn't doing it, I'm still as sober as a German judge at Octoberfest." Robyn looked around the room at some nodding heads and some perplexed looks. "Okay, you've all known each other for a long time. You've told your stories, as boys do. What haven't you talked about concerning Eirene?"

A Portuguese man answered, "We haven't talked about the actual act and what she was like in bed or the conversations we shared—or didn't. In my case, she held her sword to my throat and it became very difficult to concentrate, I tell you."

Robyn and Mark watched as everyone looked toward a man in a three-piece suit. Robyn and Mark leaned forward to see him. He was Asian with a dark complexion, short black hair, manicured hands, and blue eyes.

Robyn looked at Mark and whispered, "I'm about to call off the wedding."

Mark smiled knowingly and asked, "Should I be jealous?"

"No. I don't date older men."

The man raised his hand and introduced himself, "My name is Rayat Laut. I was born a subject of the sea. I am a free Moken. I am the oldest man at this table who has spent time with Eirene, but she did not call herself Eirene at that time."

Robyn looked at Mark and shrugged her shoulders and said, "You're in luck."

Others nodded at the man in agreement and took turns by age and described their experience and conversations, if any, until it came around to Mark.

Mark began to explain, "Well, she was ..."

Robyn interrupted, "Hey, stop there. We can all see what she's doing. She's obviously being nicer to her boy toys than in the past." Robyn looked at Mark and wagged a finger and said sternly, "I don't want to hear one single word about what she

David C. Dagley

was like in bed with you; not until I get my six-pack stomach and my womb back in my pants!"

Laughter erupted at Robyn's directness.

Gray walked in with two trays of drinks and beers. "You're a bunch of pirates! Here you go. Take them as I pass by. Robyn and Mark you're first. Take all four pints. Just so you all know, we close in two hours and none of you should drive out of here. Just saying."

The rest grabbed their drinks and wrestled for space to put them when Hong silenced the group. "We have another problem that Robyn and Mark might be able to help us out with."

Robyn and Mark put their drinks down and looked at Hong.

"It's about your friend who spent the night last night. Your children, Mark, told Eirene and she is not happy with your friend. We have to find her. She's not in your house at the moment and hasn't been since you both left for work this morning. How do you know her?"

Robyn looked at Mark and said quietly, "You're going to have to work on your parenting skills. Where's the loyalty?"

Mark explained to the group, "Her name is Kylie Hughes from Tasmania. She was our dive director when Robyn and I were on the boat and we met Eirene. They went back to go have a look because the guy that Eirene later killed had a video on his computer of the sea dragon and, maybe, Eirene. Raoul surfaced dead and Kylie never saw Chris again. Kylie has been in the cave system from land and she took something. Now she thinks Eirene wants to kill her."

143

Hong nodded, "She does want to kill her for trespassing in her domain and disrespecting her belongings. She already retrieved what Kylie stole. As for Chris, he is alive as a prisoner and she's going to feed him to the dragon after she questions him."

The Moken, Rayat Laut, cut in, "Like Robyn suggested, Eirene used to kill most of her men after boom-boom."

Gray walked in with a bill in his hand, "Hong, it's time to sort this out." He handed the bill to Hong. "Shall I run it?"

"Yes, please."

Gray nodded and walked back out.

Mark nudged Robyn before they stood up. Mark put his hands together and bowed his head. "It was nice meeting you all and we want to thank each and everyone here. Hong, thank you for this. It was insightful. We can walk home from here. There is no point in going back to the bookstore after all those beers. The cops would wonder why we're not dead. We can cab it tomorrow morning. Let's do this again some time. Hong, I'll see you soon."

Hong nodded and shook Mark's hand. "I'll come see you tomorrow at the bookstore."

"Great. I look forward to it."

Those that could stand did and said their farewells.

Robyn added, "And don't forget this weekend in Las Vegas. We have Elvis marrying us. It would be an honor to have you there, I think." She waved and followed Mark out.

Gray walked in with the credit card slip to be signed, "You guys out?"

"Yeah. Thanks Gray. We'll see you soon."

"Yep. Good night. Crawl safely."

The front door closed behind Robyn and Mark. They walked up to the corner shop and Mark walked in, leading Robyn.

Robyn was shocked. "Really? You want more? Okay, you're buying. I can't believe you threw Kylie under the bus like that."

Mark grabbed a six-pack of Sierra Nevada, two whites, two red wines, he walked toward the counter and glanced at Robyn, "They would have found out the truth eventually and then we would not be trusted ever again. Think about that. And besides." Mark put his goods down, grabbed a pen and paper and wrote: *Check for listening devices in your pockets, collar, where ever. I think they broke into our house and placed some there too. We have to talk about work, your gift, the night, things they know. Kylie is still there.* Mark finished his sentence, "I wouldn't want to give them the wrong idea."

Robyn read it in disbelief and began searching herself and found a small round object and held it in her hand and again looked at Mark in shock as he held up another. They put them back where they found them.

The clerk made change, bagged it up and pushed it to Mark, watching them curiously.

Robyn was slack-jawed and wrote down, *How do you know she's still there?*

Mark wrote down, *She was eyeing our crawl space door last night.* After Robyn read it, Mark crumpled up the note and put it in his pocket.

Robyn and Mark walked out silently and headed home. In front of the pub, Rayat Laut stood in the shadows watching them head up the street to their flat.

Mark interrupted the silence, "That was crazy meeting all those people."

A bit dazed, Robyn replied, "Yeah, I'm still trying to process it all. At least we've got our witnesses. Gray was right, they are a bunch of pirates."

Mark opened the door. "What do you really think of your present?"

"I love it, Mark. It's going to be a good thing for us now that I'm a Land-ma. What a name."

"It suits you. Speaking of which, I was kind of expecting to see a few of the kids tonight but since it's not raining they couldn't make it. Come on." Mark closed and locked the door behind Robyn.

At the top of the stairs, Robyn turned around and took the bag from Mark, "Here, I'll take that. I'm not sleepy yet. Why don't you put on some music? Or a movie? Up to you."

"Yep, alright. How about an action movie?"

"Sounds good. Half those guys tonight could make an action movie out of their embellished stories. I think they've told it so many times, they believe it." Robyn walked into the kitchen, put the beer and white wine in the fridge, and grabbed the broom as Mark found a movie channel. He clicked it and sat on the sofa watching Robyn signaling to open the crawl space door with the broom handle.

Mark nodded and put a finger to his lips.

On Robyn's way to the bathroom, she dropped the crawl space door, caught the ladder as it slid down, and set it quietly on a throw rug. She walked into the bathroom and left the door open and announced, "It was thoughtful of you to buy Kylie wine even though she's not here. I wouldn't be either if I had people chasing me and watching the house." Robyn didn't flush the toilet and walked out looking up into the darkness.

Kylie's face appeared.

Robyn put her finger to her lips and showed her the listening device from her pocket.

Kylie nodded.

Robyn motioned for Kylie to come down and pointed at the bathroom.

Wide-eyed, Kylie nodded.

Robyn moved to the kitchen and poured a red wine, a white wine, and pulled a cold beer from the fridge. She walked into the living room and put them on the table. "I think the lonely old geezer across the street has watched us enough. Do you mind if I close the drapes?"

"No. Go ahead. And we can dim the lights and pretend we are in a movie theater."

"What did you pick?"

"Have you seen the second Top Gun movie, Maverick?"

"I didn't know there was one."

"People say it's better than the first but that's not really saying much. He's entertaining. I like him better as Jack Reacher except that he's too short and not built like a barn door like the character in the books."

Robyn went to a desk and opened a drawer to grab a notepad, broke it in three sections, and picked up three pens. She moved to the bathroom door and handed Kylie pen and paper and pointed toward the living room.

Kylie flushed the toilet, followed Robyn into the living room and sat down on the couch with pen and paper in hand.

Robyn handed Kylie a wine.

Kylie began to scribble franticly as Mark explained, "Apparently, there's a lot of jet engine noise in this movie. It might be kind of loud at times. I hate movies where the dialogue is so quiet you have to turn up the volume to hear it and then a gun, a bomb, or the symphony breaks strings and goes off so loud it shakes the foundation, and you have to turn the volume down until it passes. It's annoying."

"Whatever. The jet engines will be better than the acting bits." Robyn smirked.

As the movie started, all three of them began writing on their notepads. Mark handed his note to Robyn. Robyn read it and crumpled it up while showing him the same note she had written, *What happened here today?* Mark nodded. Robyn passed her note to Kylie.

Kylie passed her note to Mark.

Mark read it. *Is she here?*

Mark shook his head and passed the note to Robyn.

The movie started out quietly with Maverick testing a jet for Mach speed.

Kylie rubbed her stomach.

Robyn got it and said, "Let's get pizza again, but maybe different toppings tonight."

Mark replied, "That'll be two nights in a row. How about a delivery from somewhere else?"

Kylie held up a note. *Fish and chips?*

Robyn nodded and said to Mark, "Yeah, too much, huh? How about a seafood place?"

"Or a steak place, or Mexican food? Bambino's has twenty-four-hour take-out and delivery. They make great burritos."

Kylie nodded.

"Burritos it is. Sounds good. I want a shredded beef one." Robyn looked at Kylie still nodding approval. "And I'll get an extra one for work tomorrow."

Kylie handed Mark a note as he spoke, "I'll make the call. I have their number on my phone." He read the note. *People came in your flat after you both went to work. I think they were looking for me. When they didn't find me, they bugged your house. Who are they?* Kylie began scribbling another note.

Mark handed Kylie's note to Robyn who read it. Robyn looked at Mark who shook his head ever so slightly while Kylie was busy writing. He raised his shoulders as if to say, *I don't know.* Mark got up and walked around the living room and began looking for Bambino's phone number.

Robyn wrote a note to Kylie and passed it over, *We don't know but there are more than two of them for sure. They follow Mark and me to and from work.*

Mark talked on his phone. "Hi, yes, I'd like a delivery. Yes. Two shredded beef burritos and a chicken burrito with extra guacamole and extra salsa."

"I love avocadoes. Can we add guacamole dip with spicy chips?" Robyn took the note Kylie had written, *Chris escaped and is alive. He's on his way here. I don't know when, but he's running for his life. I gave him your address and told him my story.*

Mark continued, "And can we get one order of guacamole with spicy chips? Great."

Robyn passed the note on to Mark who read it dumbfounded. "My name? Chris. Sorry, my name is Mark. The address is 515 Masonic. Yeah, come up Fulton until you get to Masonic. You'll see the red door. And how much? Thanks. Twenty minutes, no problem. Muchas gracias. Buenos noches."

I need more wine." Robyn waited as Kylie drained her glass.

The movie blared in the background; Maverick was being sent back to Top Gun. Jets roared up the airstrip.

Robyn moved on to the kitchen and swilled the dregs in her glass before pouring Kylie's and refilling her own. Robyn set her hands on the counter with her mouth gapping in disbelief, trying to grasp the depth of their dilemma that just compounded in her living room. She couldn't fathom the anger and hatred Eirene was carrying. She knew she couldn't tell Kylie a word, for her own sake and Mark just wouldn't.

21

The Moon and stars lit up the night sky above when the sea dragon swiftly launched out of the water onto the sand beach in the cave as Eirene dismounted mid-air. Four dolphins chattered urgently at the entrance and plunged out of the cave. Eirene instantly realized Chris's dive gear was gone. She ran up through the labyrinth to where Chris should have been lying sound asleep and saw nothing but his seaweed bonds. Eirene's roar of rage and frustration echoed through the entire labyrinth as she ran back down to the dragon waiting, poised to take her out of the cave. The four dolphins had returned and were bobbing in the water waiting for instructions. Eirene rubbed the dragon's back and looked at the dolphins and simply said, "Take me there." Eirene ran and leapt into the water and palmed two dolphins by the tips of their mouths, and they bolted out of the cave with the sea dragon loyally following.

Made, the elder in the village where Chris had been, woke up abruptly and said under his breath, "Nyi Roro Kidul." He got out of bed, put on his clothes and walked back out to the nightly fire pit. He rekindled the flames and added more wood. He collected two plastic chairs and sat in one and waited. The fire grew into a blaze of light with sparks rising into the night sky like shooting stars. It wasn't long before he could hear dolphins, and he watched as Eirene walked out of the sea. She came straight for him. Made looked around the village to make sure no one was awake or out of their huts. Eirene approached the fire and Made gestured to the chair beside him and spoke in his native tongue, predating Bahasa Indonesian. He spoke softly, "Nyi Roro Kidul. I knew you were down there."

Eirene responded in the same language, "Smart boy. I haven't heard your tongue in a long time. You've seen some days."

"Yes. I taught the whole village to speak the language of our ancestors and told them the stories so the ancestors would not be forgotten. My elders told me the stories of when the Dutch massacred our village chiefs and left us without guidance. The Dutch took our fish, our jungle hardwoods that we made our boats from, our women were forced to sleep with them, and the Dutch left us in poverty. I witnessed the barbarian Japanese when they did the same, but more brutally, taking our fish, rice, coconuts, raping our young girls, and leaving us again starving on the beach."

"I'm sorry for your people, but you survived."

Made nodded and replied, "Just. Many died of starvation and sickness. We had to start over. My father and I made sea salt to trade for food from the passing ships. We tied bags of salt to a line and they would drop meat or something that had gone off. We took it anyway and cooked it into broth to add to small fish, rice and coconut. Young girls got pregnant with half Japanese babies and no possibility of marriage. They were cast out because of the memories connected to the time and hardship."

"Yes, sad times. More to the point; you know why I have come."

Made explained truthfully, the only way he imagined he could save his people, "He was here. His name is Chris. Two of our fishermen saw him swimming in the sea near your domain with no ship. They pulled him out and brought him here to rest and eat. He told his story, but never mentioned you or what he knew. He left yesterday morning for town to get home."

Eirene looked out at the dolphins swimming back and forth, silently watching the flames and the two talking. "And where is his home?"

Made grabbed a stick and started pushing the burning wood ends into the center of the fire. "He never said where he was going, but he's American, if that helps."

Eirene pulled out her sword and began helping Made push the wood toward the center. "It does help. Thank you." She paused, looking into the embers. "How did you know I was coming?"

Made shook his head, "I didn't. But when the American showed up, I knew something bad was coming. I know when my village and my people are in danger and if I can save them with my life, I will."

Eirene nodded and concluded, "You're an honorable man, Made. You have saved your village and now I must go."

Made nodded back and added, "Please protect my village. They honor and respect you and give you your space. They are scared of you. They don't know what you are and that makes them superstitious. They turn to the spirits for answers."

"Good. Let's hope they stay that way, for their sake." Eirene got up and started walking back to the sea then stopped, turned, and looked deep into Made's eyes, "I'm sorry about killing your father. He was a good fisherman, too good." She walked into the sea and vanished.

Made bowed his head slightly and smiled contently while raising his stick, as if to say goodbye. With the long awaited knowledge and closure of his father's disappearance and death, Made sat staring into the flames as they began to dwindle along with the heat. Time passed and the Earth spun beneath the stars. The flames turned to wavering embers. Made slumped over in his chair and passed away peacefully with only the Moon and stars as witnesses.

22

Robyn lay in bed watching Mark sleep. She followed the contours in his face and figured he lost fifteen years of wear and tear. His skin was clear without a blemish. Mark's muscles were proportionately toned. She raised the sheet cover and admired his six-pack stomach.

Mark woke up. "What are you doing?"

"I'm just looking and I'm pissed off."

"Why?"

Robyn pouted sarcastically, "You look fifteen years younger and have a perfect body, and all I got was a drafting table."

Mark chuckled. "Be patient, it's coming as long as we play our part."

Robyn punched Mark softly in the shoulder, "You better play your cards right in Vegas." Robyn got out of bed and headed for the bathroom. She lifted her shirt in the mirror and saw a soft white underbelly. She threw the shirt back down, walked back into the hallway, and glanced up at the closed crawl space door before returning to the bedroom. She sat next to Mark and asked quietly, "What are we going to do?"

Mark put a finger to his lips. "We've got to get to work. But first I need to shower and brush my teeth. I smell like a brewery and you smell like everything horrible. Come on, join me." He nudged Robyn to move, led her into the bathroom, then helped her take off her night shirt and he took off his own tee shirt. He pointed at the shower. "Get in."

Robyn nodded, removed her pajama bottoms, turned on the shower, and waited for a hint of warmth before stepping in.

Mark closed the bathroom door behind himself. Their voices were now muffled by the bathroom acoustics and shower spray as they washed.

Again Mark put his finger to his lips and said softly, "We can't tell Kylie anything. If we do, we will both be on Eirene's hit list and we didn't come all this way to die."

Robyn looked worried and whispered back, "I know, I know, but what can we do? I don't know how to save them. Eirene's boy toy band is all over us. They've been going to our bar. They put listening devices on us, probably trackers too. They've broken into our house. They have the money, the skill, and the upper hand. What do we have? Nothing."

Mark handed Robyn the soap and turned around so she could wash his back. "Let's go to work and you come over when your time is up at the office and let's set you up in the bookshop like nothing has happened. Let's think about it. But remember, the bookstore is probably bugged too. Something will come up."

"What about Kylie? She can't stay in the crawl space all day."

Mark replied, "She did yesterday. If we're lucky, she may have already left."

The doorbell rang.

Mark turned around to rinse off the soap. "Let's get ready for work. I'll see to the door."

Robyn joked, "What? You don't want them to see me like this? You ungrateful bastard."

Mark got out and closed the shower door. While reaching for a towel, the doorbell rang again. "Honestly, who rings a doorbell at six-thirty in the morning?"

Robyn replied snidely, "It's probably that tart."

"It's not raining. Hurry up." Mark quickly put on his clothes, walked out of the bathroom, and closed the door behind him. He went downstairs to the door but slowed, knowing it was Hong, but the feeling wasn't the same. It was more of a warning, like he felt in the bar with the mob of pirates the night before. Whatever Hong was doing there, was not in Robyn's and his favor. He looked through the door sight and saw Hong standing outside cradling a white bakery bag. Mark opened the door and asked, "Do you know what time it is? We're getting ready for work. Couldn't it wait?"

Hong smiled and apologized, "Good morning. Sorry for yet another intrusion. I just thought I'd take you to your car after a coffee and a pastry. Can I come in?"

"Of course. Come on in. Robyn is still getting ready but she'll be out shortly." Mark walked up first, turned into the kitchen and started a kettle of water.

From the bedroom, Robyn asked, "Who is it?"

Mark's intuition kicked in and suspected the worst. With his back to Hong, he put a tea bag in a cup, slid it behind the toaster and announced, "It's Hong with some coffee and pastries." Mark grabbed three small plates from the cupboard and helped Hong distribute the coffees and pastries.

"Good morning, Hong. Do you realize what time it is?"

Hong replied, "Yes. Sorry. Mark, do you mind if I use your bathroom?"

"No, go ahead. It's just there." Mark pointed across the hallway. "I'll go check on Robyn." Mark opened the bathroom door for Hong and steam billowed out as he walked down the hall to the bedroom. "Robyn, are you ready for a pastry and coffee? Hong wants to take us to our car. You okay with that?"

Robyn said quietly, "Not really. Why couldn't he meet us later?"

"I asked the same question. Come on, let's get the show on the road. You can do your final touches at the bookstore." Mark pointed down the hall and rotated his open hand back and forth, giving Robyn the dive sign that something is not right.

Robyn nodded and followed Mark into the kitchen, and she sat next to Hong, reached for her coffee, and took a sip. "Thank you for bringing us this lavish breakfast at six-thirty in the morning, Hong." Robyn smiled politely and had another sip. Hong drank from his cup, watching Robyn.

Mark watched Hong's eyes.

Hong looked at Mark and asked, "Have you tried your coffee?"

"Not yet, it's too hot. Give it a minute."

Robyn glanced at Mark.

Hong looked out toward the living room and began to walk. "How long have you two lived here?"

Mark followed Hong into the living room and replied, "Oh, a couple years now. The house was bought and something came up for the owners so we rented it from them. I think they had to go somewhere to take care of a family member." Mark headed back into the kitchen and looked at Robyn.

Robyn pointed at the coffee and rolled her open hand back and forth.

Mark nodded and switched cups and pastries with Hong then ripped a piece of his pastry off, wrapped it in a napkin and threw it in the garbage. Robyn felt dizzy.

Hong came down the hallway and asked, "Where does the ceiling door go?"

Marked explained, "It's a crawl space. We store stuff up there to get rid of the clutter."

"May I look?"

"Help yourself. Just pull down on the latch and a ladder will slide to you." Mark looked at Robyn who now sat with her elbows on the counter and she asked, "This is great coffee. What shop did you go to?"

Hong set the ladder on the ground and looked up into the darkness. He climbed the ladder and searched the space with a pen light. Seeing nothing, he climbed down and came into the kitchen. He grabbed his cup, "The one down the road from here." He bit into his pastry and had a sip of coffee.

Mark asked, "Why would you want to see what's in our crawl space?"

Hong admitted, "We have reason to believe that your friend was here last night when you got home. We searched the house while you were at work, then again when we had drinks with you at the bar, and we still didn't find her."

With a puzzled look, Mark replied, "What are you saying?"

Hong reached into his coat pocket and pulled out all their written notes from last night and dropped them on the counter.

Mark looked at Hong and shook his head, "You broke into our house? Last night? Again?" Mark pulled out the audio/tracker and tossed it on the counter.

Hong sipped his coffee patiently as Mark reached for his tea.

Hong watched, "You didn't drink your coffee?"

Robyn slurred her words, "He doesn't drink coffee."

Mark took a sip of his tea and watched Hong look at his own cup. Mark stated, "You broke into my house three times."

"No, not me. A different group of us do our reconnaissance. But, yes, we needed to know if we could trust you."

Robyn started sliding off the counter and Mark caught her before she hit her head on the floor. Mark left her on the floor.

Hong looked at Mark. "Very clever of you to change cups but the pastry is also laced and we will all end up on the floor together when they arrive."

Mark asked, "They?"

Hong began to slur his words and lean on the counter, "We need your help. We need to make this right by Eirene. We mean you or Robyn no harm."

Mark was angry. "We'll see who is lying on the floor when they arrive. Now you have all pissed me off and I don't take kindly to breaking and entering or you drugging my fiancée for whatever reason."

Hong got off his stool with trouble and staggered back to the wall and slid down to sit hunched on the floor. His eyes closed and his head drooped as he slowly toppled over on his side.

Mark collected all the notes Hong had dropped on the counter and checked Hong's pockets. He took Hong's phone and all the money in his wallet. He threw the notes in the fireplace and burned them. Mark moved to the hall and climbed up the ladder quickly. "Kylie, we have to go. Now!"

There was no answer.

"Kylie? Your cover's blown. They know you're here. We're leaving now. More will be here any minute."

Mark climbed down and grabbed Robyn by the shoulders and dragged her into their bedroom. He went out, got her backpack and his and moved back to the bedroom to collect their valuables, wallets, passports, money on the dresser, a camera and their jackets. He opened the bedroom window and moved out onto the fire escape platform and released the escape ladder. It hit the ground with a clang. Mark dropped their bags and went back in and collected Robyn. Once on the ground, he carried Robyn and their gear out to the street and waved down a taxi.

Kylie watched from the rooftop as Mark and Robyn got in a taxi.

Rayat Laut watched from Robyn and Mark's bedroom window.

Kylie swung down off the roof drain pipe and onto the fire escape landing.

Rayat Laut wrapped his arm around Kylie's neck from inside the window.

Kylie froze in shock and fear and blurted, "I haven't said anything."

"Good. Won't you come in." Rayat Laut dragged Kylie backward over the windowsill and into the bedroom. With one hand, he dropped the window and locked it, then continued dragging Kylie backward into the kitchen and put her on a stool.

Kylie looked around and saw Rayat Laut standing behind her and then saw Hong limp on the floor. "Is he dead?"

"No, just drugged. Don't drink the coffee or eat the pastries." Rayat Laut began throwing away the pastries and pouring out the coffee and throwing the cups in the bin and continued, "We've been looking for you, Kylie, since you stole something from a very influential person and fled Indonesia. We are going to wait for this man to wake up. Meanwhile, you are going to tell me everything from the beginning. This doesn't have to get ugly, but it will if you don't cooperate. Cup of tea?" Rayat Laut filled the kettle, turned it on, leaned against the sink counter, crossed his arms and legs and waited.

Mark and Robyn sat in the back seat of the taxi. Thirty minutes had passed and Robyn still hadn't woken up.

The taxi driver periodically looked in his rearview mirror and asked, "What's wrong with her?"

Mark replied with a smirk, "She mistakenly took a sleeping pill instead of a multivitamin. We're supposed to be flying to Vegas tomorrow, so I thought I'd get her to a hotel close to the airport and start our holiday. She'll be fine. We're engaged to be married."

"Oh, congratulations, I think." The taxi driver chuckled. "How long have you two been together?"

"Five plus years."

The driver nodded, "Then you know what you're getting into."

Mark brushed back Robyn's hair and nodded, "Yeah, I do. Can you think of a hotel near the airport with a shuttle?"

"Yeah. I got you covered. There's a Fly-Bye with a shuttle to the airport."

Mark hopped on his phone and looked up Fly-Bye SFO Airport and called the number.

Robyn began to stir, hearing Mark's voice, and she reached for him.

"Hey, Robyn. Are you waking up? We're in a taxi, heading for a hotel near the airport so we can fly to Vegas. Are you good with that?"

Robyn opened her eyes, looked at Mark, and spoke lethargically. "Oh, now you're in a hurry to get married. What the hell happened?"

Mark winked at Robyn and explained, "You took a sleeping pill instead of a multivitamin with your coffee. I figured we'd take advantage of the time."

Robyn sat up slowly and used her sleeve to wipe off some drool from her mouth. "Fine. And here I was hoping you'd take advantage of me with a date rape drug before we got married. So much for fantasies."

Realizing all was well, the taxi driver laughed.

Robyn continued, "And so much for my new computer and filing cabinet delivery."

Mark assured Robyn, "I'll make that call when we get to the hotel. Then we can talk."

"I need coffee—real coffee." Robyn grabbed Mark by the hand. She looked in the rearview mirror at the taxi driver's eyes and added, "Isn't he a catch?"

"Ah, I think he caught you this morning. No more pills today. At least, not until you get to Vegas." The taxi driver smiled. "We are almost to the hotel."

Hong moved cautiously and saw Rayat Laut and Kylie talking at the kitchen counter. Still feeling the effects of the drug, he stood up, holding onto the counter.

Rayat Laut looked at him. "Ah, you're awake. Kylie and I have been rehashing what happened in Indonesia. How are you feeling?"

"Not great, but it'll pass. I didn't ingest that much." Hong reached into his pocket, searching for his phone. "Mark took my phone. Can you put a trace on it?"

"Let me just call it first." Rayat Laut pulled out his phone and called Hong's number.

Robyn was on the hotel bed calling work for a sick day when Hong's phone rang. Mark put it on speaker and said, "I was wondering when you'd call."

"Hello Mark. This is Rayat Laut. Where are you?"

"In a hotel making arrangements for our trip to Vegas. You guys still coming? We moved it up a day considering the circumstances of you all breaking into our house, listening in on us, and trying to drug us."

Rayat Laut agreed, "We will see what we can do about Vegas. Hong just woke up from a hangover. You tricked him. Good on you."

"Yeah, well, he deserved it. Are you still in my house with Hong?"

"Yeah, Hong, me, and your friend Kylie. She's been filling me in on what happened in Indonesia and after. It's not her fault, but Eirene is pissed and looking for blood."

Robyn asked angrily, "What's with all the listening devices in our house and why drug us? That's bullshit!"

Hong came closer and spoke, "As I told you earlier, we weren't after either of you. We needed to find Kylie and now, apparently, Chris, who has escaped from Eirene, is on his way here in the next couple of days. According to your notes we read and the noises on the listening devices, we assumed Kylie was here. The drugs were to keep you here until she revealed herself. We do not want to harm Kylie or Chris, but we can't stop Eirene. We need to resolve this situation quickly. And I'm going to need my phone back, if you don't mind."

Mark replied, "I'll put it in a taxi and have it delivered to my address. Now what's going to happen?"

Rayat Laut cut in, "Me and some of the lads will go to the airport and watch for Chris. Kylie and Hong will stay here and mind her phone. Can Kylie use your bedroom?"

Robyn looked at Mark and replied. "Of course she can. Just don't harm her."

Hong replied, "We have no intention of harming her, but we have another problem. A couple of your children, Mark, are on both sides of your house under the drainage grates. Movement for us has to be stealthy. Let us know when the wedding is and some of us will attend. Some of us will not be able to make it due to our present situation."

"Okay. We are going to go about our business. And I want to thank you, Hong, for the lavish wedding gift." Mark pulled a wad of hundred dollar bills out of his pocket and dropped them on the bed in front of Robyn.

Hong looked puzzled. "What wedding gift? I haven't given it to you yet."

Robyn put her hand over her mouth covering a huge smile and replied, "Oh, but you did. It looks like Mark emptied your wallet." Robyn laughed and added, "Thank you so much for invading our privacy, breaking into my house a couple times, bugging it, tracking us, drugging me, and kidnapping our friend. That was very generous of you. And now Mark doesn't have to stand on a corner in Vegas." Mark and Robyn smiled at each other.

Hong reached for his wallet and felt it empty. He smiled. "Fine. That should tide you over for the long weekend. You are welcome. I'll give you your other present when you return."

23

Eirene listened to the music and watched from outside the sea swells and beach break as the villagers cremated Made, the elder. As she watched the revolution of life once again, a large sea dragon approached quietly and touched Eirene's sea dragon, nose to nose.

A man's head surfaced next to Eirene and whispered, "Hello, sister."

"Hello Triton. Haven't seen you on the surface for a while. How's the deep?" Eirene continued watching the villagers as they gathered Made's ashes and put them in an urn. The murmur of cymbals, drums and praying chants carried over the sea.

Triton shrugged his shoulders and replied, "It's quieter than up here, for sure. All we get is whale song. None of this clanging racket."

Eirene looked at her brother, "Why are you here?"

"I heard Made call for you and thought I'd come say hello and pay my respects. I also hear you have reason to pay respects."

Eirene nodded. "It was a long time ago and his father was fishing in the wrong place for the wrong fish at the wrong time." Eirene paused remembering Made's father and continued, "I sat with Made at that very fire pit recently. We had a short conversation about where a certain person drifted off to. He spoke in an old tongue."

Triton watched as the villagers put Made's urn on a floating platform adorned with flower arrangements. Some villagers brought trays of food and others brought money and placed it all on the float. "You've got a problem with a human or two. I'm here to help, if you need it."

"Thanks, but I've got this. It's nothing serious but keep your eyes and ears open. Let me know if they get back on or in the sea." Changing the subject Eirene asked, "How's Father?"

"Good. He's in the trenches off the Galapagos. He's protecting the Ecuadorian coast guard vessels who are trying to stop the Chinese from illegally fishing. It's bad. We've lost a lot of sharks and other endangered marine species to Chinese greed. Their day will come."

"Good. I've got to go to California and clean this up. I'm waiting for two people to marry and return to the coast so I can talk to them. They are my easiest connection to the couple who broke into my house. Some of my children are watching them and keeping me posted. Give Made safe passage, will you." Eirene swam backwards away from Triton.

"I will. Call out if you need me."

"Thanks. Will do. Until next time and say hello to Father for me." Eirene wrapped her arm around her sea dragon's neck and disappeared under the surface.

Triton calmed the sea as the villagers prayed and walked the float out into deeper water and set it adrift. The villagers returned to the beach and watched the float, prayed to the gods, sang their songs, and bid their farewells. Triton guided the float out to sea where it drifted beyond sight and eventually sank and set Made's spirit free.

24

Chris landed at San Francisco International with only a carry-on, he headed out to get a SIM card and call an Uber to get into the city. Men followed him loosely as he got in the car and drove off. He called Kylie to let her know he was coming.

As Chris arrived at Mark and Robyn's flat, he looked up to the window and saw Kylie waving at him but not smiling. He gave her an okay sign and she responded with a wavering hand but motioned him in nonetheless.

Chris went to the door and Hong opened it from inside and greeted him, "Welcome to San Francisco, Chris. Won't you come in?"

Two men came up the stairs behind Chris blocking his escape. Chris asked, "What's going on? Who are you?"

Hong stepped aside to allow Chris in. "Come inside and all will be explained. We mean you no harm, but there is one who might and we are trying to resolve the problem before one or two people get killed. Please, come in."

Kylie stood at the top of the stairs looking down with her arms folded, "Come up Chris. We don't have a choice at this point."

Chris walked up the stairs, dropped his bag on the landing, and saw more men sitting around the living room, and heard people in the kitchen.

Hong spoke up, "Did you have a pleasant flight?"

Chris shook his head slightly, "Not really. Too much on my mind to get much sleep. What's going on here?"

Hong went straight to the point, "Apparently, you had a run-in with an acquaintance of ours and one of your friends was killed. I'm sorry about that. You were captured. Kylie snuck in and out another way, stole an item, then you escaped, and our friend is coming for you. She wants to silence you."

Chris nodded, "All that happened and we have been running ever since. How do you all know her?"

Hong replied, "That's a long story and we don't have time to explain. What we need to know is if you told anyone else?"

Chris shook his head, "No. Nobody would believe me."

Hong asked, "And video. Did you take any more videos?"

Kylie responded, "The only one with a camera was Raoul and he didn't come back with his camera, at least not when I pulled his body out of the ocean. There is only the one video clip that we looked at on Raoul's computer and now it's gone with his belongings to his family in Buenos Aires, Brazil."

Two men got up and walked down the stairs and left the building.

Chris watched them leave. "Where are they going?"

Hong looked at Chris and answered, "Buenos Aires."

Chris looked around the room nervously and asked, "Okay. You have us. Now what?"

Hong explained, "Your choices are limited. If you run, it's certain death. The second choice still has a strong possibility of death, but not certain. You both would have to go back to see her. Chris, you would dive down and enter the cave and wait for her. Kylie, you would go back to the atoll to the hidden entrance and wait for her there.

Kylie asked, "What if we go to the desert where she can't get to us?"

Rayat Laut stood up and came over to Kylie and explained "Her family is not only in the water. Some can walk on land as we do. They will find you and kill you without mercy. You would be looking over your shoulder for the rest of your short life."

Kylie spoke up. "I'm still connected to the live-a-board company, but we wouldn't be able to hire the boat in time. We could rent one maybe?"

Rayat Laut looked around the room at approving nods and stated, "We have boats. All of us are experienced sailors, not divers. We can get you there and anybody else who saw the video."

Kylie and Chris said nothing of Sari and Sophie.

An Irish man sitting on the couch added, "Plus, someone has to drink that aged whiskey. Wouldn't want it to go bad after all these years."

The others chuckled in agreement and randomly mentioned, "Or the beer."

"Or the wine."

"Or the opium."

Hong came forward and asked, "You two will go back and face her then? An apology of innocent curiosity would be a good start." Hong looked at Kylie and Chris. "But it probably won't save you."

Chris and Kylie looked at each other and Chris stated, "We have no choice."

"It's settled then. Kylie, pack up your gear. We will charter a flight to Maumere and travel by car to Larantuka, where we will board our ship. Let's get busy and tell the others to get ready."

Kylie went to Mark and Robyn's room and began to pack while the others who knew their part in the expedition left. Only Hong and Rayat Laut remained. Chris went to the refrigerator and grabbed a beer and sat down.

Rayat Laut went over to Hong and quietly asked, "And who is left to talk to her when she comes?"

Hong whispered, "Mark and Robyn will convey the message. She's on her way here now. I called Mark and explained everything. The ship should be at Eirene's doorstep before she arrives. The crew will protect Kylie because she is the only one among them that knows the surface entrance."

25

Back home in San Francisco, Mark opened his eyes and looked over at Robyn. Her eyes were wide open staring back at him when he asked, "Did you hear that?"

"I did," said Robyn.

"What was it?"

"I don't know."

Mark sat up with his feet on the floor and looked at his watch. Four-thirty a.m. He grabbed a pair of jeans and a tee shirt off the floor. Robyn got up and went to the bathroom. Mark walked to the window, looked down at the backyard and the neighboring house, and watched the shadows. He moved to the living room and looked down along the street.

Robyn turned on the kettle and came out in pajama bottoms and a sweatshirt, tiptoeing across the cold wood floor to Mark's side. An eerie dolphin song filled their heads. Mark winced and Robyn covered her ears. The shrill sound took Mark back to memory fragments of feeling the current pull him down, falling through the water, the dragon with a jaw full of hooks, the woman under the sea, sleeping with Eirene, the treasury, bloodied logbook pages splashed across his mind, wandering aimlessly through the labyrinth, and the constant echoes of dripping water.

Robyn's memory put her onboard the Eolian to the moment Eirene pressed her against the door and threatened her life at sword point. Robyn could see Eirene clear as day and could hear her say: *It's time to talk.* Robyn announced to Mark, "It's her." The dolphin whistles faded away and Robyn looked at Mark and said calmly, "It's her. We have to go to the beach."

Mark looked over the buildings across the street toward the Pacific Ocean and replied, "I know. I'm thinking."

Robyn reached out and took Mark by the forearms and confidently argued, "Mark, she's not trying to kill us. She's trying to communicate. She's calling us. I need to meet her." More loudly she reiterated, "Mark. I need to meet her."

"I know, but that's also part of the problem, there are no others here. It's just us."

"Eirene didn't kill Hong and she's not going to kill us. You're not going scuba diving; you're going to the beach. You have to. Let's get dressed and I'll drive. Come on. The kettle is on." Robyn slowly walked backwards, still holding Mark as she moved toward their bedroom. Mark knew she was right and followed her willingly.

Robyn moved to her dresser drawers and opened the middle drawer and asked, "Which beach should we go to?"

Mark opened his closet doors and stood with his eyes closed. "It's not the closest beach. They're in the fog. At this early hour, that would be Muir Beach or Bo-Bo. They are secluded." Mark searched his thoughts and continued, "They recently passed Point Reyes and Bodega Bay and," Mark chuckled and added, "a couple of the kids scared the snot out of an old fisherman in the lagoon." Mark laughed.

175

Robyn looked at Mark as she put on a windbreaker and exclaimed, "They? How come it's always they?"

"Yeah. There are some of my children coming and maybe somebody else's. I can't read them like I can my own." Mark put on a sweatshirt and a baseball cap as he moved toward the kitchen to make tea.

Robyn poured coffee grounds out of a bag and said, "Well, don't you think we should meet them? Say hello at least?"

Mark dropped a tea bag in his cup and a spoonful of sugar and explained, "I can hear them, Robyn, but they're not all here."

Robyn added, "So can I, well, not them, just her. She says we need to talk and I told her we were coming."

Mark stopped at the top of the stairs loosely palming the banister and calmly agreed, "Yeah, we're coming."

Robyn came out of the kitchen with her cup and asked, "Do you remember the night she brought you back on board the boat and put you in Caroline's bed?"

Mark walked slowly down the stairs, "Not really."

"She told me this day was coming, as long as I said nothing."

Mark stopped at the door and looked up at Robyn as she came down the stairs and replied, "You've told me that."

Robyn shrugged her shoulders and smiled as she gently pushed Mark out the door. "Let's go."

Mark and Robyn drove north across the Golden Gate Bridge. San Francisco and the bridge were under a rushing current of thick fog and wind and the orange lights of the bridge dripped diagonally. They drove above Sausalito on the

101 and exited at the Tam Junction turnoff to Muir Woods. The road ran against the mountainside, up into a eucalyptus grove, and further up to an intersection locally known as Four Corners. The mountain ridge and bushes were carved by the wind while the fog continued to surge down the mountainside into Mill Valley. The winding road down to Muir Woods was wet and dark with only their headlights revealing misty cliffs, guardrails, and the intermittent yellow line in the middle of the road. Mark and Robyn drove silently, pondering what was going to happen after five years of nerve-racking fear for Mark and anticipation for Robyn. There was no clear explanation of the past, present or future events. They found themselves in uncharted waters. Robyn passed the entrance to Muir Woods and continued on with bay trees, oak trees, and a wild hedgerow of poison oak and berries bordering a creek to their left and fenced pastureland above them to the right. A bobcat watched as they passed.

Robyn broke the silence, "What's going on in there?"

Mark shook his head slowly, "I really don't know what to think. None of this is normal. What if she is here to kill me?"

"Seriously? You think she swam a couple thousand miles with your kids so she could kill you in front of them? That doesn't make sense. That would leave a mark on the children, no pun intended." Robyn paused while thinking. "Just listen to them. Are they sending you death threats or greetings? I think I'm beginning to hear them, we must be getting close." Robyn turned right at a Tudor style bed and breakfast called the Pelican Inn. Mark was admiring the well-kept grounds when Robyn tapped on his arm and pointed to an opposing pasture gate where three horses stood with their heads over the rail and ears forward, watching them drive past. Blackberry bushes filled the gaps between the pine trees, and nettles covered the road down to the beach. The gate was locked and there were no other cars parked along the sides when Robyn pulled over and turned off the engine. They sat in the deep fog listening to the surf crashing in the muffled distance.

Robyn reached over to Mark's hand and held it. "I'm supposed to be here too."

"I know you're supposed to be here. How else was she going to get me back to the water? It's just that, no matter what happens, our lives will never be the same and there's no turning back."

"I understand. We are on the verge of something never before experienced by mortals, not even by those few men we met who have history with Eirene. And just to set the story straight, there was no turning back when I met you, before you were caught in the downcurrent and were taken into the labyrinth. From that point, everything you've done is either out of fear or survival and you've been living with fear for way too long. It's time to let the fear go and she has the answers and the cures, no matter the outcome."

Mark added, "Okay, since we're setting the story straight, I do have to mention that there were many others who she dealt with that were murdered by her later for whatever reason."

Robyn grew impatient. "We've gone through this, Mark. The others told us the same thing at the bar. I have as much to lose as you, me being the first female to have met her and still breathing. I just hope I don't grow a tail or something. Gills would be cool."

Thinking out loud Mark stated, "She's immortal and we're being given long life. She said it's both a curse and a blessing and it's up to us to figure out how much of each we can handle."

"On the long life thing, when was the last time you were sick? Or changed pant sizes? Or even got hurt? Mark, nothing has happened to you in five years and not that you should have noticed but I look the same as I did when you met me on the Eolian, but I'm changing. I can feel it. I still don't have my six-pack stomach and I'm still not able to have children but I'm the same woman that fell in love with you before this nymphomaniac seduced you, and I am still in love with you after all these years. All I got was a drafting table and a boy toy with no money who looks younger than me. This has to be fortuitous, so let's go see what's in store for us." Robyn knew Mark and, once again, tried to lighten the stress she could feel emanating from him. She wanted him calm immediately. As they listened to the wind and waves crash on the beach, Robyn warned, "She better not hand me a six-pack of shitty beer or I'm going to hit her with it."

Mark smiled as he opened his door and swung his legs out of the car. "Let's go." He glanced into the fog toward the beach.

Robyn pulled the keys, got out a few steps behind Mark and locked the doors. She looked back to the horses now standing behind blackberry bushes, still watching them. Mark and Robyn walked into the fogbank, following the silhouette of a tiered red earth parking lot.

As Mark approached the beach, a dolphin clicked in the surf near a grey-brown rock cliff to his right. He could vaguely see silhouettes of houses along the ridge above him to his right. Another dolphin clicked and called out at the other end of the beach, and Mark turned his head but could barely make out the grassy hillside ending in another dark cliff of rock. Waves broke out of sight and rolled into whitewash and chaos surging to the beach. The dolphins continued calling as Mark walked over the high tide cusp of the beach that now sloped into the ocean. He scanned the green-blue murky water and waves as they rose and fell. Robyn followed down the beach and snuggled under Mark's arm. They were both searching the horizon when a seal popped up between the waves. Mark pointed at it, "Look there, a seal." They removed their shoes and moved down into the dark wet sand.

As the seal grew closer, Robyn said with confidence, "That's not a seal."

"What? Yes, it is." Mark took a second look and replied in dismay, "Oh, no it isn't."

As the child swam toward them, other children surfaced and swam cautiously, keeping their distance. Robyn put her hand across her mouth with wide-eyed amazement. The closest child smiled and stared at Robyn and Mark.

Mark asked, "What do I do now?"

"Mark, you haven't been in anything but a pool in five years. You used to love the ocean and what's in it, the animals, plants, coral, all the strange evolution that takes place right here on Earth, just in a different environment. It's part of you and I think it's time you get reacquainted."

Some children nodded at Robyn and chirped and clicked to each other like dolphins. One child caught a small wave and came into the shallows and stood up slowly as small waves passed him. He looked like any other soaking wet boy on the beach on any given day. He reached out his hand and invited Mark, "Come play with us."

Mark looked at Robyn and then at the boy. Robyn let go of Mark's arm and stepped back. Mark walked forward not knowing what to expect. Mark touched the boy's hand and felt the warmth in him. A little girl appeared from under the surface and took his other hand, leading Mark out to sea fully clothed and, within minutes, all three disappeared under the surface.

Robyn stood on the beach in the wet mist holding herself, fearfully weeping and waiting for Mark to reemerge. Sea birds sang overhead, hovering in the onshore wind and approaching morning light. Time passed and Robyn squatted down. She watched as a shadow swam under the waves toward her. She held her breath and peered into the green-blue water. As the shade approached, a dolphin sounded and Eirene rose out of the water and walked to Robyn.

Robyn was half afraid of the answer when she asked, "Where's Mark?"

Eirene pointed to a boiling commotion near the breaking waves.

Robyn could see it and asked, "Is he all right?"

Eirene shrugged her shoulders and replied, "Ask him yourself when he comes out. But in the meantime, we have to talk and I have questions."

Dismayed, Robyn blurted, "You have questions?"

"Yeah, like why doesn't he ever write?" Eirene smiled and added, "Just kidding. I know Mark hasn't entered the water since he spent time with me. I can feel him when he's in the water and he hasn't been anywhere near it until this morning. Why is that?"

"True or false, he has it in his head that you intend to kill him."

Eirene nodded, "Not today. I suppose he told you why?"

Robyn looked out to sea and back at Eirene, "I think he told me everything about his time with you including you blackmailing him into bed."

"Blackmail? Is that what he called it? What else?" Eirene folded her arms.

Robyn continued, "Wandering your halls, looking through numerous logbooks with incriminating entries referring to you and the carnage you caused to numerous sailors, scuttling vessels and taking the treasures for yourself. I think, once he knew how many sailors you had killed, he thought you'd try and bury him with the truth in a watery grave. It was enough to scare him out of the water for five years."

"Not that Mark would know the difference but I sank hundreds of whaling vessels at my father's request. And if I wanted Mark dead, I'd have done it myself, I promise you that. It was not my intention to scare him but he did know some pretty personal stuff like where I live, that's the biggest secret I still want kept. All the other stuff, if he mentioned anything to anybody else, they would think him a crazy person off their meds." Eirene looked out toward Mark and continued, "I'm hoping this visit lets him know it's okay."

Robyn asked, "Is it?"

Eirene turned to look at Robyn, "Yes. Besides, the children have been nagging me to bring them here for some time. They've been watching you both. They want to know where they came from and some of the other children have never met their fathers for various reasons. They're learning whom to protect and whom to avoid. Some of us avoid all human contact but it's harder these days with so much illegal fishing, trawling, ghost nets, garbage collection systems, oh, and did I mention curious inexperienced divers like your friends, Chris and Kylie?"

"Yeah, about them. What's going to happen to them?" Robyn looked out after Mark as he broke the surface before being hammered down by a large wave.

Eirene eyed Robyn, tilted her head and stated, "You know where they are."

"Yes. Hong and Rayat Laut and a few others took them to Flores Island, to a town called Larantuka to meet a ship and set sail for your place."

Eirene looked surprised. "Hum. They call Larantuka the city of one thousand churches. Sounds like an extremely ominous reunion. When did they leave?"

"A couple days ago by plane to Labuan Bajo or Maumere. Then they plan to drive to Larantuka and set sail on a night with no moon." Robyn added, "I don't know what that means."

While Eirene was thinking of the ship, she explained, "It's called a New Moon. It envolves the Earth's rotation around the Sun and the Moon's rotation around the Earth at the same ecliptic longitude. Eirene paused for a moment before adding, "I think I'll call on my brother to slow them down and test their mariner skills, at least until I can get there. You know they're all a bunch of pirates, right? They are after the riches in my house and Kylie is the only human that knows the land entrance on the atoll. Kylie will be safe until she shows the entrance, then they'll kill her. Chris is of no use to them. Obviously, Kylie hasn't given away the details of the entrance or they wouldn't need her either."

"We were at a gathering of your past conquests and Hong mentioned the children were watching us and the house. Hong wanted to know where Kylie was, so I'm guessing you wanted Hong to find her through us. That would mean you told him and he conjured up a plan to use her to get to you. This is just a guess. Did you tell Hong about Kylie?"

Eirene recognized her mistake in trusting Hong and asked, "In your world, do you trust your lovers, partners, or men in general?"

Robyn replied, "As for past lovers, I can vaguely remember a few of their names and I certainly do not have children by any of them. As for men in general, I've trusted very few long term, my father who died and Mark are at the top of a very short list. The rest, due to betraying me one way or another, I wouldn't let hold my hand, let alone tell them anything of personal value."

"And my family wonders why I live in isolation. Men's affections, charms and loyalty can easily be swayed by greed and infected with deceit."

"Can be. It depends on the man." Robyn felt the chill of the wet fog. "When I met those men at the gathering in the city, I didn't get the impression they were all bad people, but once a few of them broke into our house and put listening devices on us, then my perspective changed. Some of them even came to celebrate our wedding." Robyn held out her hand and showed Eirene her modest ring of a diamond surrounded by smaller red rubies.

Eirene apologized, "Oh, sorry, how rude of me. Congratulations on your marriage. May it be long and fruitful. And my gift to you is you can now have children again. May I?"

To Robyn's surprise, Eirene lifted Robyn's shirt and put her hands on Robyn's abdomen.

Robyn could feel heat coming from Eirene's hands as she moved them. "Awkward."

Eirene let go and said, "Right. You're all set. You probably won't have just one, so don't be surprised, unless that's all you want is one at a time. You also get long life. Mark's children tell me you want 'that' body. Granted. All the best to you both. Just remember, you have to bury what you know deep down and never mention it to others, especially you, being the first woman I've allowed myself to know. Don't make me regret it."

"Thank you, Eirene. You won't regret it." Robyn asked, "So what now?"

"Robyn, I really hope we can be friends. I'm going to go kill a boat load of men I thought were loyal to me. They have proven themselves otherwise. And I'm going to need Mark's and your help in the future." Eirene moved toward the ocean.

"*Friends* might be pushing it, seeing as you've killed many already and I only met you once at the tip of your sword five years ago. But I'm open to new beginnings." Robyn smiled.

"I did what I had to do and I'd do it again if need be." After a few steps and splashing through the shallows, Eirene turned again and said, "Mark and my children and you and Mark's children will always be safe, hopefully growing up together, watching each other's backs. Agreed?"

Robyn felt the impossible had been granted. "Agreed."

"Don't you just love surprises?" Eirene walked backwards into the water facing Robyn and smiled. "It's nice to meet you, Robyn Tassley. You'll both have to come over and stay for a while. And if you and Mark decide to move to Flores Island, we can arrange that and I will sponsor the move financially. It's an open invitation. I'll know when you're near." Eirene dove into the surf in the opposite direction where Mark was body surfing a wave, being led by a child swimming around him.

Robyn smiled hearing Mark laughing as he came into the shallows and rolled on his back covered in sand and strands of kelp. A wave of whitewash splashed over him as he lay on the beach. With arms and legs out stretched Mark laughed and hooted. Robyn walked toward Mark as four children stood in the water to their shoulders. They stood fast as if the waves had no effect.

"There's a connection, a most incredible feeling." Mark stood up as Robyn approached.

Robyn looked at the children over Mark's cold wet shoulder and asked curiously, "How many of these children are yours?"

Mark spun around slowly and said, "Well, these four, for sure. I met them the other night across from the bar."

"That's a good round number. That tells me nothing. Let me rephrase my question. How many children total are yours?"

Mark shrugged and grinned, "I have no idea. I couldn't exactly see very well underwater or feel much, but I sense more."

"More?"

Mark shrugged with a smile and replied, "Some could have been dolphins. I could feel a group of children kept their distance and just seemed to watch but never surfaced or interacted. I had a different connection with them and they feel older and bigger. I'd say there were fifteen to twenty offspring down there, but not mine."

The children laughed and clicked amongst themselves, then began diving out to sea and swimming away. The last girl came closer with a smile on her face and said, "More."

Robyn spouted, "How many more?"

The girl looked at Mark and asked, "Where are their fathers?"

"Whose fathers?" asked Mark.

"The older children. They can't find their fathers."

Eirene shot out of the water, grabbed her daughter under her arms, began walking backwards, and said sternly, "That's enough!"

Mark and Robyn backed up onto the beach.

Eirene and her daughter plunged underwater and vanished below murky foam and turbulent waves.

Mark and Robyn looked out to sea until the dolphins headed off. Mark said quietly, "It would be nice to find their fathers."

"I can only guess what happened to them." Robyn grabbed Mark's arm, "Come on. Let's get you out of the water before you catch your death of cold."

Mark shuffled a few steps up the beach toward their shoes and chuckled quietly. He put his cold wet arm around Robyn's bare neck and said, "That's impossible."

With the shock of cold water, Robyn moved out from under Mark's soaking sweatshirt and stood like a defensive wrestler in front of him, both smiling at each other. They began snickering and teasing, chasing and tripping each other up the beach on their way back to their car not fully aware of what they had become.

26

Three fully loaded Land Rovers drove into a secluded cove near the town of Larantuka and everybody got out to stretch their legs and arch their backs. They all started staging supplies by the water's edge. When all was done, they sat together drinking as the sun set over a volcanic ridge on the west side of the bay. The sunset filled the sky with colorful glowing shades before fading into night.

A silhouette of a ship sailed silently into the bay. Kylie and Chris remained seated as a few men got up, excited to move their supplies to the ship and get underway.

The Irishman spoke up, "Right, what's the craic?"

Rayat Laut and Hong remained silent and seated, glancing at each other with knowing eyes.

An Englishman responded sarcastically to the Irishman, "Well, they're not going to row a boat over here, ya daft limey."

The Irishman looked at him and replied, "So we have time for another?"

"Knock yourself out." The Englishman grabbed a bottle of scotch.

The Irishman looked at his crate of whiskey and asked, "How long is this going to take, to get there I mean?"

The Englishman pointed at the ship and said, "Look at her. She's sleek with some subtle curves. You know the way. Figure it out."

Irish looked at the ship intently, awakening his memories of sailing back and forth from Ireland to India and India to China, running opium to blackmail and secure a port in China. He responded, "I have time. They haven't even dropped anchor."

The Englishman agreed, "The boys brought her in and turned her about, but they haven't released any skiffs or anything. We have time to down another, you worthless cur. Don't be in such a hurry."

Irish replied, "It's a windy night. We'll make good time."

Everybody relaxed and watched and waited for the telltale sound of the anchor tumbling into the sea and creating a rust cloud of flakes tearing off the corroding chain links.

The crew on the boat had their duties and were fine-tuning the trim, waiting for the captain's order as they did during their seafaring days, before Eirene changed their lives.

After the supplies and passengers boarded, the captain called out to weigh anchor and set sail. As the sails dropped and caught the wind, the ship gently keeled to one side and slid silently through the water. They peeled out of the cove and bay to the east and set more sail. There was no moon.

Hong and Rayat Laut remained on shore and sat in silence watching the ship slither into the darkness before Hong said quietly, "They were good lads."

Rayat Laut agreed, "It's still a survival situation for us. You and I have avoided certain death and I'm not sure what to make of that. We also betrayed our friends."

Hong drank from a small bottle of Soju and replied, "She has already made the call. Triton is already here and watching them."

Rayat Laut dropped his head, sat back and raised his bottle of Arak in honor of those on board the ship and both men went silent deep in their own fond memories of their companions.

The ship turned Northeast. Under full sail, the ship keeled over further and cut to its course. The ship creaked and flexed ever so slightly. Chris and Kylie stood at the bow, arm in arm, looking out over the sea, smelling the salt air and feeling the spray on their faces, both pondering what the future held for them. With death on the menu, every moment alive became acute and with purpose.

The crew went about their business, adjusting sails and making fast the lines to catch maximum wind. It was a well-seasoned ship, all teak wood with two stout masts cleated to the top deck and fastened to the keel. There was no wheelhouse, just an exposed wheel and a brass compass console. Once the ship deck was secured, most of the men went below to set up their sleeping arrangements, mostly hammocks hanging between support posts. A few men helped set up the galley, stowing supplies in the dry goods room and hanging meat in a locker, fastening pots to the stove top with clamps and securing utensils out of the way.

Irish walked up to Chris and Kylie, "A beauty of a night for a sail. Have you looked up at the stars yet? They are brighter when there's no moon to distract you from their shine."

Kylie and Chris separated and looked up at the stars. Kylie responded, "Yeah, they're amazing. I recognize a few constellations."

Irish agreed, "Oh yes, and the skipper and the first mate, the gent at the wheel, both steer by them. They know these waters without a chart as long as they can see an island mass. Once we leave the islands, out comes the sextant for positioning. These boys prefer to sail the old way. It's what they know. There is a sense of adventure rather than being guided by some electronic toys and a satellite. These men take pride in their knowledge of the sea, especially when she turns nasty. You both can learn from these lads."

Chris interrupted, "But most of you were shipwrecked. Isn't that how you met the woman?"

"Her name is Eirene and yes, that is true, but most of us were just young boys back then. It was hardly our fault. The decisions came from the captain, and still do, but most of our crews died at sea a long time ago. On another subject, I've taken the liberty of stowing your gear in your state room. Let me show you where you'll be sleeping and then go ahead and have a look about the ship, whatever."

Chris and Kylie followed Irish to their state room and looked inside and saw their gear. Chris asked Irish, "I haven't seen any tanks or a compressor. Where do you store them?"

"No worries." Irish pointed at Kylie with a smile, "We're going in with her. She knows the surface entrance. I'm going down for a feed. Come down if you want grub." Irish walked off.

Chris and Kylie walked back out to the bow. Chris surveyed the ship deck quickly and said quietly, "Something isn't right. Those other two guys, Hong and Rayat Laut, didn't get on board."

Kylie replied, "So?"

"When I was down in Eirene's place, I saw rooms full of silver, gold, pearls, all kinds of treasure. What if that's what these men are after and you're the key. With no tanks or a compressor, I'm not able to get back in the cave from the surface. I am bait for the eel or Eirene. But you Kylie, they need you to show them the way in so they can rob her and probably kill us, or she will. We have to make a decision about whose side we want to be on. If we help these pirates, she will kill us. Or ...."

"Or we help her you're saying?"

Chris nodded and replied, "Yes. Or warn her. It's truly our best option to stay alive. We have to do it together or it doesn't work. What do you want to do?"

Kylie shrugged her shoulders and stated, "We don't know what these men are planning, if they are planning anything. But, if they are, then I agree, we need to warn her. Right now, we're heading to her to apologize and still probably die, but at least we'll die knowing the sea still holds life-changing secrets."

"Kylie, that is a lovely sentiment but absolutely useless at this point. It's all or nothing now. We will need an escape plan. The easiest option is to take a skiff but we need options. Let's keep looking."

Kylie nodded and hugged Chris and said quietly, "This is all so surreal."

"I hear you. We have to stay focused or we're dead. We don't have a choice. Let's go eat and play along with the others and listen in. Eventually, we'll overhear something or they'll press you for the entrance. Irish already told us they are counting on you to get in. You can never tell them or show

193

them the entrance. Never. Not even under threat of torturing me or killing me."

"If you're right, you should escape soon and warn her. Like you said, they need me for the entrance. But they can use you against me and I won't be able to stay silent, even knowing they will kill me once they know how to get in. You must warn her, Chris."

Chris nodded and explained, "I will. When we reach Alor, I'll jump overboard when we are close enough to swim. I'm sure they'll stay between islands for weather protection. We've dived there with all the crazy marine life and local children swimming down to greet us."

Kylie shook her head. "The current can be brutal in that area. You're going to have to time it so you don't miss the islands."

"At least there are islands on both sides of the shipping lane so if all goes south, I can swim ashore opposite Alor and hire a boat taxi if I have to. Maybe she'll find me on some little village beach. But I need to eat. I haven't eaten anything but airplane food and a couple of beers in two days."

"Okay. Good idea. Let's go." Kylie moved off toward the galley and Chris followed under the watchful eyes of the first mate at the helm and a deckhand by his side. When they entered the galley, the crew went silent.

The cook got up and made two plates of food and handed them to Chris and Kylie. The crew made room for them to sit.

27

Mark and Robyn arrived home in San Francisco and went in. Robyn walked off to the shower and Mark peeled off his wet clothes and put them in the washer. He put on board shorts and came to the bathroom door, knocking before entering. "Hey." He opened the shower door and looked into Robyn's eyes and asked, "What do you think?"

Robyn was washing her hair. She glanced back at Mark, knowing what he was asking and replied, "I don't know."

"There's got to be something we can do."

Kylie explained, "It's off season. We'd have to hire our own boat."

Mark nodded. "I know a few dive companies still that might be able to help us. They could supply the boat and be on their way in a day or two to meet us in Larantuka or better yet, Alor. It's closer to the trench. Or we can hire or borrow a boat ourselves."

Robyn added, "And airline tickets?"

"SFO to Jakarta, get through immigration and fly domestic to Maumere or Alor, whichever one gets us to our boat."

Robyn leaned forward and began rinsing her hair. She asked, "And who's going to pay for all this? We didn't exactly earn bragging rights in Vegas."

Mark replied, "I think Eirene will be happy to pay for our aid."

"And I'll probably get fired from my job."

"Start your own company at the bookstore. Maybe we can buy the lease from your uncle."

"He owns the property, and yeah, we could talk to him. Again, it's a matter of time and money. We're not taking out any stupid loans in this economic volatility shit storm leading into a recession." Robyn paused in thought before continuing, "Mark, at first, I wanted to go help too, straight away. That was my first thought. Then I asked myself, what do we actually gain by going? This is not our fight. We would be putting ourselves right back in harm's way and I just got a physical upgrade I'd like to enjoy before I get stabbed with a sword. I seriously doubt Eirene would be happy to see us considering it's not our battle. How many weeks are we talking? A month? Longer? I would definitely lose my job and the bookstore would be closed for most, if not all, the time we're gone." Robyn turned off the water and wrung out her hair. Mark handed her a towel as she continued, "My mind warns me not to go. I feel our part in this is over and Chris and Kylie made up their minds and are heading to Eirene now. I don't mind looking at our possibilities. I can look at airfares and you deal with the boat boys. Keep in mind, the crew cannot know our true destination. We are going to have to work on that. On second thought, I'm afraid and I don't want us to go. Plus, I don't think we can catch them. You take a shower. I'll put some food together and let's talk about it."

Mark's phone rang and he went into the kitchen to get it. Looking at the name and number he answered it, "Hong? I thought you set sail for Eirene's place?"

"Hello Mark. The ship has set sail with Kylie and Chris on board. Myself and Rayat Laut did not board. We are still in Larantuka and wanted to give you a heads up. By no means should you try and rescue your friends. We suspect the crew has ill motives. We think they are going to take Eirene's treasure and possibly fight her. Your friends will surely die if they don't get off that ship and we couldn't say anything to them without someone possibly overhearing. The only thing you can do is send them a phone message and hope the crew has not taken their phones away. Do you have Chris's or Kylie's number?"

"I don't but Robyn does. Robyn agrees with you. We were just talking about that and Robyn has a bad feeling, and I trust her."

Robyn walked into the kitchen with an inquisitive look on her face.

Mark put the phone on the counter and turned on the speaker. "You're on speaker so Robyn can hear this."

"Eirene and her brother will kill all who remain on that ship, especially if it reaches the channel. You can warn Chris and Kylie, if you want, but I cannot. I don't know if it will help, but it's worth a try."

Robyn chimed in, "I spoke with Eirene this morning. She knows Kylie and Chris are on the ship and on their way from Larantuka. She also suspects a fight. She said she was going to call her brother to slow them down until she gets there."

Hong replied, "She has already made the call, and she has a few brothers and sisters and you do not want to tangle with any of them, ever. She most likely will call on Triton. He's the closest, I think."

Robyn got out her phone and searched for Kylie's number to send her a message.

28

A night had passed and Alor was on the evening horizon when Kylie was finally within tower distance and got the message from Robyn.

The captain's mate watched Kylie's phone glow. She read the message. The mate watched as Kylie turned back and looked up at him. She walked below, out of sight toward her cabin where Chris was reading a book.

Chris looked up at Kylie's face and saw her concern. "Hey. What's up?"

Kylie whispered, "I just got a message from Robyn and you were right. Hong called and explained that these guys are up to something. She said, if we remain on the boat, we will die. We have to go, now. We are near Alor bay on the far side and the other islands are closer."

Chris closed his book and reached under the bed and pulled out a dry bag with his valuables and his fins and mask. "How many people are on deck?"

Kylie thought about it and replied, "The mate is at the wheel and a deckhand is wandering about but mostly at the bow watching for debris and obstacles."

"Then we go to the stern. We can't use the skiffs because they're secured with a lock and key. We must swim for it."

Kylie nodded and grabbed her dry bag, put it over her shoulder and head, and turned out the light as they quietly left the cabin. Chris locked the cabin door from the outside before they crept off.

Chris peered out and saw the deckhand standing on the bow holding the forward jib line, looking out to sea. The ship was dark and the crew were mostly sleeping or drinking below deck. Chris led Kylie to the stern rail where they climbed overboard and dropped silently into the water and darkness. They treaded water while watching the ship as long as possible before they began swimming for the closest island. They could barely see the island's silhouette. The current was swift as they swam side by side.

Time passed before Chris heard an engine approaching. He grabbed Kylie and stopped her. Chris spoke quietly, "We have to separate. You continue swimming for the shore and I'll go with the current. I'll see you again. I love you. Now swim like your life depends on it and don't splash. If they get close, swim under water as much as you can. Do what it takes to stay alive. They're coming for you, not me."

Kylie pulled her mask down around her neck shaking her head and weeping, knowing Chris was right. She kissed Chris and demanded, "Find me." She swam off toward the closest beach.

Chris swam freestyle on the surface, kicking and splashing, following the current and not trying to hide. As the skiff approached, their search light tagged Chris and came straight for him. One of the men on the skiff fired a gun at Chris and caught him in the shoulder. The skiff ran over Chris as he took a deep breath attempting to dive below but was cut by the propeller before he went under and disappeared. The skiff circled back looking for his body but only found a cloud of blood.

Kylie watched as the skiff circled with the spotlight beaming into the water and then she swam quietly toward shore. When Kylie reached the shallows, she was pulled back into the sea and never surfaced.

TWO YEARS LATER

29

Robyn and Mark had moved out of San Francisco, across the Golden Gate Bridge, to a quiet neighborhood in the redwoods at the bottom of a valley with a small creek running through their property. They were playing in the pool with their two-year-old twins.

Robyn smiled at Mark and spoke to the twins, "Okay, let's see how long you can hold your breath one more time, then we're done with lessons for the day."

Mark looked at his watch. "One, two, three, go."

The two children dropped under water as Mark hit his timer. The children didn't go to the bottom and sit, they swam together the length of the pool, turned and swam back and continued. They clicked at each other like their step-brothers and sisters. They swam breaststroke fashion, finishing with a dolphin kick for momentum and glide.

Mark and Robyn looked at each other after getting a feeling that someone was near and coming to the house.

Hong and Rayat Laut walked down the side of the house for the first time in two years. Hong knocked on the corner and asked, "Mind if we come in?"

Mark waved them in. "Welcome. We were wondering when you would show up."

Rayat Laut waved and bowed his head slightly. "Hello Robyn and Mark."

Mark looked to the children still swimming back and forth underwater then at his watch still ticking along.

Rayat Laut and Hong sat at a wood table in the shade of an umbrella.

Robyn looked at Mark and asked, "You have your eye on them?"

"Both."

Robyn stepped out of the pool and asked, "Welcome. Would you boys like a cold beer or anything?"

Hong nodded. "That would be great. Thank you."

"Mark?"

"Yes, please. And maybe some juice."

Hong watched Robyn walk into the house. Her body had changed and she was blessed with both physical strength and beauty. Hong looked at Mark and asked, "Have you been in touch with Eirene much? We know she's been around but she hasn't made contact. Actually, I've only spoken to her once quite recently. She said you had a child."

The two children popped up.

Mark stopped his watch. "You two are awesome! You're learning. Lessons are over for today. Come meet your uncles."

The two children clicked and Mark nodded. The children swam under Mark's arms and wrapped their legs around his waist on opposite sides and looked at Hong and Rayat Laut.

Rayat Laut got up and walked slowly to the edge of the pool and knelt down to look at the children. He saw their florescent blues eyes then looked back to Hong and quietly said, "They're pure."

Robyn came out with her hands full. "Yep, and since they were born, in the rainy season, the other children come and play with them, teaching them their language, and taught them to swim before they could walk. The others even spend the night in the pool on a rainy occasion." Robyn handed Rayat Laut a beer as he got up from the edge of the pool. She handed Hong a beer to and moved to the pool stairs where she sat with her wine. The children swam over to her effortlessly for their juice. Mark followed and Robyn handed him a beer.

Rayat Laut shook his head. "Amazing. They are part of the next generation."

Robyn nodded and corrected him, "They *are* the next generation."

Hong corrected Robyn, "Yes, but they are not the only two."

Mark asked, "What do you mean?"

Rayat Laut explained, "When you got married, we took Kylie and Chris to Larantuka where they set sail for Eirene's home. We didn't get on board. Chris's intuition kicked in and he became suspicious before Robyn's message got through. They snuck off the boat and attempted to swim to shore. The crew came after them and shot Chris. Triton grabbed Kylie for her protection because, if she had gone to shore, the crew would have certainly captured her and forced her to guide them to the hidden entrance. Chris drifted in the current and was later found by Eirene. He explained everything and warned her before he passed out. Eirene and Triton conjured up a storm and swell that broke the ship into pieces and sea dragons ate the crew. They won't have to eat again for a couple years. Eirene took Chris back to the labyrinth to mend for a week or so. Meanwhile, Triton decided to educate Kylie on what humans have done to the oceans and show her from below. Since they were in Indonesia, he showed her how third world countries with meager garbage disposal systems handle garbage, mostly by throwing it in creeks, illegal dump sites or dry river beds. When the rainy season comes, run-off pushes all the garbage down rivers and creeks, kills all the fresh water fish in its path and all the rubbish and dirty nappies purge into the ocean. He showed her what should be pristine beaches look like buried in plastic debris, flip-flops, chunks of Styrofoam, everything you can imagine that floats and is not biodegradable. He showed her examples of toxic waste purging into seas and oceans from the global industrial complex. They swam through the radioactive contamination from Fukushima Daiichi Nuclear Power Plant in Japan where they recently started letting all the cooling water into the ocean. Triton took her off the north coast of France and showed her the scuttled German submarines, other sunken vessels with leaking fuel tanks, oils, and Freon. She now recognizes the extent of this global pollution killing coral, taking away juvenile marine life habitat around the world and having an adverse effect on marine life in general. Skin diseases are becoming common and sensitive marine life is now often born abnormally with more and more lesions and tumors. Triton also took her on a tour to show her what tragedies the commercial vessels, trawlers, and poachers have done to marine species. They witnessed the killing cove of Taiji, Japan to show her the brutal and gruesome slaughtering of dolphins and other marine mammal species. They sell some dolphins into a life of prison and slavery in marine parks around the world for human entertainment. The majority of dolphins are killed and the cove turns red. Kylie witnessed how humans are killing everything above and below the oceans. She has become a true warrior of the sea. Wait until you talk to her. She's not the same." Rayat Laut and Hong finished their beers and stood up to leave.

Robyn stood up and asked, "So, she's alive?"

Hong turned and added, "And has been given gifts similar to yours, Robyn. There are some differences but, yeah, she's alive and learning the ways of the sea. None of this would have happened without you two."

Mark blurted, "And Chris?"

Hong replied, "Yes, he's alive. They'll be in touch." Hong and Rayat Laut walked toward the walkway around the corner of the house and Hong stopped and turned around. "I forgot to ask. What are your children's names?"

Robyn pointed and stated, "That's Chris and that's Kylie, in honor of our friends we don't want to forget."

Rayat Laut and Hong laughed heartily and Hong replied, "That's going to get difficult later because Chris and Kylie have two children, a little younger than yours. The boy is named Mark and the girl is named Robyn. In honor of those who saved them." Hong waved, "Until next time."

We'd like to know if you enjoyed the book. Please consider leaving a review on the platform from which you purchased the book

Printed in the USA
CPSIA information can be obtained
at www.ICGtesting.com
JSHW080332290723
45575JS00006B/54